Human Oddities

Human Oddities

[*Stories*]

Noria Jablonski

Shoemaker & Hoard

"Succor" first appeared in *Faultline*.

Library of Congress Cataloging-in-Publication Data
Jablonski, Noria.
Human oddities : stories / Noria Jablonski.
p. cm.
ISBN (10): 1-59376-084-1 (alk. paper)
ISBN (13): 978-1-59376-084-7
I. Title.
PS3610.A337H86 2005
813'.6—dc22
2005010498

Book design by Mark McGarry, Texas Type & Book Works
Set in Palatino

Printed in the United States of America

Shoemaker 〔S&H〕 Hoard
An Imprint of Avalon Publishing Group, Inc.
Distributed by Publishers Group West

10 9 8 7 6 5 4 3 2 1

For my father,
in memory

CONTENTS

One

Pam Calls Her Mother on Five-Cent Sundays   3
Succor   19
The Good Life   32

Two

Big Guy   45
Solo in the Spotlight   56
The Monkey's Paw   60
Wanting Out   67
One of Us   83
The End of Everything   106

Human Oddities

ONE

Pam Calls Her Mother on Five–Cent Sundays

PAM calls her mother on five-cent Sundays, so Sunday afternoon she called her from bed. When she admitted that she'd taken to bed, her mother said, "You did it again, didn't you?"

"Did what?" said Pam.

"Listened in," she said. "To Jim."

"I don't want to talk about it."

When her husband, Jim, moved out, Pam bought him an answering machine, a housewarming gift for his new apartment. This machine had a special feature, a room monitor ("Honest to God," Pam said when she first confessed to her mother about the spying, "I didn't know about the room monitor till after I bought it"). You dialed the number, and when the machine picked up, you pressed 5 to hear messages. But if you pressed 6, the machine became a room monitor with a very powerful built-in microphone.

This would not make a good spying device unless the person who owned the machine was totally ignorant of its functions. That was the case with Jim. All he had to do was read the instructions, like Pam did before she gave it to him.

The only problem was that the machine beeped every so often while she listened, and whatever woman Jim had over would go, What is that sound? and Jim would say, Oh my answering machine, it does that. Sometimes the voices were muffled, like Jim had put a pillow or something over the machine to quiet the beeping.

Her mother said, "Are you going to your support group? Women Who Love the Men Who Hit Them?"

"Women Who Love Too Much," said Pam. "I couldn't find a group in my area. I did try a Sex and Love Addicts Anonymous meeting, but they were all compulsive masturbators, and all men." She pulled the Band-Aid hat off her thumb and scrutinized the cracked yellowing nail lifting off its nail bed. It wouldn't grow normally because of all the shampooing; Pam did hair for a living, and her thumbnail fungus thrived on the wetness. "I *am* an addict, Mom. Jim's an addiction. A disease. He's like a splinter in the tip of my finger that got infected, and now I have to cut my whole arm off, that's what it feels like."

Her mother said, "I have to have the six giant pines in my yard removed. It's rather sickening, like going bald. On the bright side, I'll get full sun all year. Of course most of my plants will probably burn up."

"You could get new trees," said Pam. "I'd fly down and help you plant them."

"Sure, I can get new trees, but it'll take years for them to grow big. These trees are forty years old. My homeowner's insurance will pay five of the six thousand it's going to cost because the trees are going to fall. They're invested with bore beetles."

"Infested."

"The workmen will probably trample all my flowers. My neighbor's as upset as I am—it's her afternoon shade. At least now I can grow tomatoes. At least there's that."

Pam rolled the ball of her nose, making the cartilage pop. "The woman at Jim's last night was singing show tunes. Show tunes! Ha! He hates musicals."

"I knew it! You *were* spying on him, and that's why you're upset."

"I'm an addict," said Pam, working her cartilage faster. "I don't want to talk about this. Jim's not why I'm depressed, Mother. I'm sad because an old lady died yesterday at the shop. Client of Sandy's."

"Which one is Sandy?"

"My boss. Not my boss actually, my owner." She reached for the clock to turn it so she could read the numbers: 2:27. Eventually, she would have to get out of bed to meet her four o'clock at the shop for his perm. Gerald liked the red rods, the littlest ones Pam called Barbie perm rods. "I was the one that found her."

"Sandy?"

"Her client. Olive," said Pam. "I gave her mouth-to-mouth."

"I didn't know you knew CPR."

"I don't. But she was dead already anyway." *I think,* thought Pam. "I had my mouth on the mouth of a dead person—that's why I'm feeling blue. Not Jim." Then she sang what Jim's date had sung, "The sun'll come out tomorrow, bet your bottom dollar that to-mor-rooow there'll be—"

"What's the weather doing up there?" her mother said.

"Gorgeous. The sun finally came out yesterday."

"We've got your rain now."

Pam said, "Something else—something strange, good-strange—happened yesterday, too. After I'd finished with Mary—"

"Who's Mary?"

"My regular—she never tips. After Mary, I went to the bathroom to wash up and walked in on Sandy shaving. Her face."

"Well, I guess that is strange," her mother said.

"No, no. I haven't gotten to the strange part. I'm setting a mood. So, I come out of the bathroom, ready to head over to the Funeatery for salad bar, and there they are—walk-ins, twins, identical twins. I'd guess they were in their seventies. Eighties? Come to think of it, I've hardly ever seen old lady twins before, or maybe I just haven't seen them *together*."

"Except for the gals that worked at Millie's Chili Bar," her mother said. "Remember? Those two were so fat, three hundred pounds at least, each, with matching gray bob haircuts, and pointy cat-eye glasses—what a sight!"

Pam said, "These two, even though they're in their seventies, maybe eighties, they dressed like little girls, like you dressed when you were a girl, Mom, in these old-fashion party dresses. Lilac ruffles with big green cabbage roses, ostrich feather fringe around the hem. And tights and tap shoes. They looked like a birthday cake."

"Yes, that sure is strange."

"Don who I work with was rolling a spiral perm on his client, Moira. She's a nurse. Pretty. Could maybe be a model except for those white bumps on her eyelids. Don shoots me such a look and starts singing, 'I've written a letter to Daddy. His address is heaven above,' you know, from that Bette Davis movie."

"I don't know."

"You do, you just don't remember," said Pam. "Don's funny. He seems gay but he's not—he tried it but he didn't like it. Now he's with Sheila the manicurist. They got their hair frosted to match, and they're both fat, huge. We're all fat at Hair We Are. A bunch of butterball roly-polies." Pam paused, interpreting the silence on the line as an affirmation of her fatness. "Sandy's small on top, but she's got the biggest hips I've ever seen. Compared to all them, I'm tiny." She stopped talking. Waited for her mother to say something, but apparently she'd set down the phone. Pam heard the sounds of putter. After several minutes, she hung up.

Pam introduced herself, and one twin said, how do you do? The twin said she was Fern and that, she jerked her head, was Rose.

"What pretty dresses those are," Pam said to say something.

Rose pinked and Fern laughed, "What, these? Honey, these are our old show clothes! We got caught in that bitter, bitter cold rain last night—pajamas and these affairs are all we've got that's dry, and we can't go pounding the pavement in pajamas."

"Show clothes?" said Don, folding a perm paper over the ends of the short hairs at Moira's nape. "You gals in a show?"

Darkly, Rose spoke. "We were in a show. Lots of shows."

Fern changed the subject. "So, Miss Pam, think you can make us pretty? Are we too tall an order?"

Pam asked what did they want exactly, shampoo-sets, haircuts, a color?

"Something to fluff us up a bit," said Fern.

"Something not too pricey," said Rose.

Pam said, "Whichever of you is going first should go on back to the sinks and maybe whichever of you is going second would like a *manicure* while you wait." She said it loud so Sheila could hear what a valiant effort she was making to drum her up some business.

"We couldn't afford a manicure," said Rose. The way she said it, Pam felt terrible for bringing it up.

Fern said, changing the subject again, "Normally, we have a girl who comes to us. We never go to beauty parlors because we can't sit in the chair, so I'm not sure how you want to do this. What's easiest for you, Miss Pam?"

"What do you mean can't sit in the chair?"

"See," said Fern, "because we're attached."

Pam had assumed they were standing close together, arms linked, sisters joined at the hip. What she saw now was that they were literally joined at the hip. Pam said, "Well. This complicates things, yes indeedy."

Don whistled through the gap in his teeth and said, "Siamese twins! The real deal!"

"*Conjoined* twins," Nurse Moira corrected him.

With Fern leading, the twins clipped across the floor, sort of sideways, crabwalking to the sinks. Sandy poked her head out the bathroom door, a pearl of shaving cream adorning her earlobe. "What about Siamese—oh!"

Then the front door opened, and it was Evelyn and her mother, Sandy's one o'clock, Olive. Evelyn was old so her mother must've been ancient, somewhere in her nineties at least. Olive was a smaller, grayer, more powdery version of Evelyn. Olive walked in a slow underwater way with a pair of orthopedic canes with four prongs like midget table legs on the bottoms.

Evelyn said bye, she'd be back after she did errands. Sandy loudly asked Olive how she was today. "I had cheese toasts for lunch," said Olive. "I only eat cheese toasts."

Pam shampooed Fern and Rose, who were fine at the chairs at the sinks—those chairs didn't have armrests. She was thinking about her mother, how her mother was still bitter about childbirth, as if it were something Pam did to her on purpose. *I wonder how she'd have felt if she birthed a Fern and Rose. I wonder how I'd have felt if I'd done that.*

With the skin of their faces pulling back smooth while Pam massaged their scalps, she could see what beauties Fern and Rose had been. Such fine bones. Such thin skin, roadmaps of purpley red veins showing on their eyelids, and a bluish vein Pam thought at first was a bruise—then she thought it was smudged makeup until she tried to rub it off—underneath each of their right eyes.

Toweling anyone's hair dry is a motherly thing to do, but drying the twins' two heads, Pam felt especially motherlike. Then she shuddered, imagining what a C-section was like back in the day when Fern and Rose were born.

Don was squirting perm solution on Nurse Moira's head, and it smelled like burning. Moira was saying how usually she works in pediatrics and she likes that because they only have "clean kids" at her hospital—appendectomies, tonsillectomies, none terminal, nothing too depressing. But yesterday, she said, she was a "floater" on another ward and she had a gory experience but she won't say what because she doesn't want to spoil anyone's lunch. No, no! Tell us, they all said (except Olive who was there but seemed to be elsewhere). *What Romans*, thought Pam, *hungry for blood we are. Blood and circuses—ooh, that's clever!*

A diabetic foot was what grossed-out Moira. Young guy, handsome, she said, who'd had his toes amputated because of a foot infection. Moira said if you're diabetic you're prone to infections but you can't feel when you've got an infection. Her job was to pull out the old dressing and pack his foot full of new gauze. His foot was concave as if his toes had been scooped out. She said she kept saying, This might hurt, and he kept saying, Nope, I can't feel it.

Pam knew all about packing from when she had a tummy tuck. She'd had complications. She got a tummy tuck because a) she'd always been self-conscious about her middle, and

b) with her second, her son, she got so big she thought he might be twins.

Her belly got so big one day she burst, her stretchmarks stretched, the skin tore and bled, and even though she rubbed it religiously with cocoa butter and vitamin E, her belly stayed loose, all puckery like a deflated balloon.

When her father died, she could finally afford plastic surgery. She had the operation just after Jim left for the trial separation. Several days into her recovery, she laughed too hard, so hard her stitches split. But they don't stitch you back up. Instead they pack you with gauze. They showed her how to do it to herself, so three times a day she had to pull out the old packing, which was like ripping something out of her stomach because it sticks, it scabs to you inside, and then cram herself full of sterile gauze over and over for days.

"Can I ask you a personal question," she asked Fern and Rose, whom she'd sat on stacks of phone books on ordinary chairs, same as she used to have her kids sit for their haircuts. She combed out the twins' wet white hair.

"How do we do it?" said Fern.

"What?"

"How we do it, hon," Fern winked at her. "Sex." Rose gave Fern a disapproving swat.

Of course, Pam was dying to know, but she said, "No, no. I wonder what brings you—here. You have family here?"

Fern said, "We don't, and we didn't pick here—"

"Here picked us," said Rose.

"It's a lo-ong story," said Fern.

"A tale of woe," said Rose.

They all (not Olive) said tell us, tell us. Like a musical, like a cue to break into song.

"Six weeks ago or so," Fern began, "we got a call. Fellow by the name of Farwell, John Wayne Farwell. He said there was going to be a revival of our films—"

"Films?" said Don, eyebrows up.

"*Freakshow* and *Bound for Life*. You wouldn't know them," said Rose.

"Before your time," said Fern. "And banned, besides."

"I do know," said Don. "You're the Hyatt sisters!"

"None other," said Fern.

"In the flesh," said Rose.

Fern said, "Mr. Farwell told us he'd arranged to show the pictures and would we like to come, do a little number."

"We need the money," said Rose.

"We got in last night, raring to go for our big comeback. That fellow Farwell promised to meet us at the Greyhound station."

"Let me guess," said Pam. "No John Wayne Farwell."

"No. No John Wayne Farwell. And no John Wayne Farwell in the phone book either," said Fern.

Don said, "Criminals always have three names like that."

"We figured there must've been some misunderstanding," said Fern. "Maybe our Mr. Farwell was meeting us at the theater. At the Mystic."

"Oh no! The Mystic's been closed for what, two years?" said Don.

Fern said, "Girl at the bus station told us the theater was just two blocks away and we thought, hooray! On with the show! Then we saw the newspapered ticket booth and a padlocked chain."

"Then it started to rain," said Rose.

They'd spent the last of their Social Security for this month on the bus ride. They didn't even have money for a motel. What they did have were saxophones, and Harmony Music, two doors down from the Mystic, was open late. So they pawned their saxes to pay for a room at the Peter Pan Motel. Pam couldn't stand the idea of them staying at the Peter Pan, a pay-by-the-hour place by the freeway, though Fern and Rose said you can pay by the week too. They said the prostitutes there are very well-mannered.

Anyway, there wasn't anything for them to go home to, just a fruit stand that failed because the peaches this year all had black spots from too much rain. Fern said, "There's nothing wrong with them, really, but who wants spotty peaches?"

"People get nervous about spots," said Rose. Apparently peaches were the main draw at their fruit stand, peaches and soft serve. But the ice cream machine exploded. After that, they just gave up.

"If we could," said Fern, "we'd go back to being show folks. But live shows are kaput. People look down on them. Also, they're so expensive to run. Now, if you're lucky, maybe you'll get a two-headed baby pickled in a jar—"

"Or a five-legged cow," said Rose.

"Or one of those kids with a unicorn horn," said Fern, "and some old pictures tacked up on the side of a tent."

"Pictures of us," said Rose.

"Kids with horns?" said Pam. "Really?"

Fern laughed. "*Goats.* Though our friend Sammy, rest in peace, really did have a horn."

"Gristly thing coming out of his cheek," said Rose.

"So here we are," said Fern. At Hair We Are, spending what precious little cash they have to get their hair done, so they can find jobs, so they can make enough money to recoup their saxophones.

By this time, Pam had finished setting their hair in rollers, so she sat the twins under the dryers. Don drizzled neutralizer on Nurse Moira's perm, which stops the hair from melting, which made the shop smell delicious, like green apples. Pam went for a Coffee Nip in her purse to have something sweet to suck on. She keeps candy in her purse, same as her mother. In her underwear drawer too, just like her mother.

After Sandy put Olive under a dryer, Pam asked if Sandy's ex, Alan, still managed Carl's Corner Market. Assistant manager, Sandy said. Pam had seen a sign painted on the window, *having fun is contagious—help wanted* with smiling lips and teeth that made the whole thing look somehow dental.

Sandy hung up the phone and said Alan could see the twins ASAP. Nurse Moira volunteered to drive them over to the interview. Under the orange heat lamps most people look ridiculous, but Moira looked regal almost, a science fiction movie queen, Empress of Mars. Don helped Pam take out the twins' clips and rollers, then he backcombed and sprayed Fern while she did Rose, and Sandy teased Olive's hair into a pale blue-rinse cloud.

After they told the twins the news, Fern wanted to know was Sandy still friendly with her ex-husband, and Sandy said practically best friends. Pam stage-whispered, "Alan's gay." Then Fern asked Pam what about her, was she married. "Divorced," she said. "We're not friends."

"Good riddance to bad rubbish," said Fern, like she knew.

Pam didn't show the Polaroids of herself all black-and-blue that she keeps in her purse. At first, she showed those pictures to everyone, but everyone acted like she was the crazy one for showing them the pictures, so she stopped talking about it anymore and she stopped showing the pictures.

Don said, "We're all gay divorcées."

"I'm not divorced," said Sheila the manicurist.

Fern said she'd been married too, but it was a sham marriage, just for show. She said she was engaged once, for real, to a dancer, but their marriage license was turned down in twenty-one states, nobody would perform the ceremony.

"Give us a kiss," Fern said to Don, tilting her cheek and tapping it. "For luck."

When Don kissed Fern, Rose sighed dramatically and feigned a swoon, like she was the one who'd been kissed.

Fern and Rose tipped Pam ten dollars, which she said was too much but they wouldn't take it back. Outside, the salon staff helped the twins into the backseat of Moira's Jeep and waved after them until they were just a champagne-colored dot on the expressway.

"Their mother sold them when they were babies," said Don. "Sold them to a couple who treated them like chattel and beat them."

Sheila said, "What's chattel?"

"Slaves," said Pam.

"Just like Patty Duke," said Sandy, "in her book *Call Me Anna.*"

Suddenly the salon was so empty, quiet except for the scritch-scritch of Sheila filing her nails.

For the second time that day, Pam was on her way to lunch. She had to wait her turn for the bathroom, to get that sticky sheen of hairspray off her hands, because Olive was in there. Don was giving Sheila a neckrub, and Sandy sat at her station, smoking a long brown cigarette. Ten minutes Pam waited, fifteen. "Fifteen minutes is a long time," she said, chewing her lip, "for a person to take in the bathroom."

Don said, "Pfft. Fifteen minutes is nothing."

Pam rinsed her hands with the nozzle at one of the shampooing sinks, using a dab of shampoo for soap. She put a fresh dry Band-Aid on her Frankenstein thumb. Then she knocked on the bathroom door. "Olive?" she said, knocking louder and jiggling the knob. "Olive!" She announced that she was going to break the door down.

"And what if the door bashes into her? Or lands on top of her?" said Don. He unbent a bobby pin, lowered himself to his knees, and probed the hole in the doorknob. He couldn't get the lock to click.

Throwing her shoulder against the door, Pam made a hollow thud. She backed up and ran, buzzing with adrenaline, and hurled herself at the door again. That didn't work, so she kicked—*hi-yah!*—cracking the doorframe, and the door gave in.

Olive was facedown on the floor. Pam rolled her onto her back and she was blue. Blue hair, blue shocked-open eyes, blue like Pam had heard of; she'd never seen a person actually be blue, but Olive was. Pam pinched her nose closed and blew into her mouth five times. Olive's skin next to hers was downy soft and so cold. Pam sat up and put one hand over the other and push, push, pushed on her chest, then put her ear there and listened. The ambulance took twenty minutes to arrive. Olive's daughter Evelyn pulled up as they were carting her mother away under a sheet.

"They are cutting the trees down now," said Pam's mother, on another Sunday, "and I don't feel nearly as bad as I thought I would. There is an upside. I can grow tomatoes, and no more climbing up to the roof to get pine needles out of the downspout holes."

Pam said, "I could fly down and help you plant tomatoes."

"And I can see stars from my bedroom window. Last night I was lying in bed, thinking what're those? I put on my glasses and—wow!—stars."

"Last night I went to flick a grain of rice off the countertop and the rice moved," said Pam. "I saw another one, then one more dropped down onto the counter and I looked up and the ceiling was covered with little wriggling white worms."

"Meal moths," her mother said. "Or weevils. Or maybe they're the same thing."

"I inspected cereal boxes, crackers, flour—webby, all of it. And a whole confetti of bugs flew up out of the instant pudding—the pudding's the culprit—then there was no point in inspecting anymore, they were everywhere in everything. So I threw away all my dry goods, which were stale anyway—so much of the food's been here since before Jim left." *Good riddance to bad rubbish,* she thought.

She didn't tell her mother that after the moths she'd dialed Jim's machine. No sound. Kept calling until three in the morning, compulsively listening—no sound. *Yep, he's truly my heroin.* If he'd been there, even if he were sleeping, she'd have heard him breathing. He breathed like a beast.

"Or," said Pam, "I've bought too much of a thing because I still haven't figured out how to shop for just myself."

"After your father died, I always bought too much, too."

"Today I'm shopping for new food at the Carl's Corner," said Pam. "It's clear across town, but the twins are there. I never did tell you about the twins."

"You told me already about the twins," her mother said. "They looked like a cake. Fancy."

"They were Siamese, Mom. The Hyatt sisters, Fern and Rose. Maybe you remember them."

"No, my parents didn't take me to see that sort of thing. My parents were Unitarians. Isn't it strange how we're both invested with bugs? What're the chances?"

"Yes, Mother," Pam said in a tight voice. "That sure is strange."

○

Carl's Corner smelled funny, sort of gamey, but there was clapping, people clapping together in rhythm, and singing. By the corral of shopping carts, Pam watched Fern ringing up groceries while Rose bagged, cans on the bottom, bread on top, and everyone in their line clapped along as Fern sang, "You've got two nice arms—"

"You've got two arms too," piped Rose, gaily.

Then both sang, "Let's put two and two together."

"You've got two blue eyes—"

"You've got two eyes too." Clap, clap!

"Let's put two and two together. The single mode of living may seem a lot of fun, but when it comes to loving, two heads are better than one."

"You've got two red lips—"

"You've got two lips too."

"Let's put two and two together!" And they kissed on the lips lightly to applause.

At the checkout, Fern and Rose came out from behind the counter and drew Pam into a hug. Bay leaves, they said when she told them about her moths, bay leaves would do the trick. They hiked up their tied-together aprons, then promenaded jauntily in a small circle, like a pony, showing off their new dress, one of several that Alan had bought them. Alan beamed like a proud papa from the customer service desk.

"Good old Alan," said Pam when she phoned her mother again that afternoon, "he sure is dull and not too good-looking, but his heart's in the right place."

Pam sang some of the song, and this time her mother remembered. They were on the radio. She'd seen them in the paper, young, jazzy, with sausage curls and saxophones. They were the same age as her and very pretty. Out of the blue, she said something about Pam being the pretty one in their family.

"You always used to tell me I was fat," said Pam, "that I was too fat around the middle. You never once told me I was pretty."

"You used to turn heads! People stared! I didn't want you to get big-headed about it."

Pam called her daughter, Valerie, and told her what Grandma said. Valerie let out a poof of air and said, "Last time I saw Grandma, she said I actually looked kind of pretty—she actually said *actually*."

"I always told you you're beautiful," Pam reminded her.

"Yes, but you were lying," said Valerie.

Yes, but.

When Nurse Moira came to the shop to have her perm redone in the front where it'd gone flat, she asked had they heard about the twins. Flouncing onto Don's chair, she said, "Fern had a stroke and Rose called 911." Don Velcroed a cape around her neck. "Rose's heart kept pumping blood into Fern, but Fern was already dead, so her heart couldn't pump the blood back." As Don jacked the chair with his foot, Moira went up, up, up. "Rose's blood pooled up inside Fern. Rose bled to death."

Pam shut herself into the bathroom, slid the wastebasket in front of the door to keep it closed because it wouldn't close properly or lock since she broke it down. The blood was up in her ears, burning behind her eyes, throat tightened around a ball of breath: all the right conditions for crying, but no tears came. She sat on the toilet and saw her reflection in the doorknob.

She laughed, what else could she do.

Succor

THE front door opens with a suck-pop. Inside it smells like scrambled eggs and peach, fake peach. "Hello-o?"

A stilted chorus of hi's comes back at me, and an *unh* sound. My mother.

"Look at you!" my mother's mother greets me in the living room. "You actually look kind of pretty."

The drapes are closed. Grandma's perched at one end of the sectional sofa; next to her is my younger brother, who is alarmingly thin, all shoulders and elbows, his head much too large for the rest of his body; Mom's wrapped in a snarl of blankets, propped up on pillows. She's wearing tinted glasses that give her fly eyes. What I can see of her face isn't nearly as swollen as I thought it would be, but it's orange and waxy-looking. I lean to kiss the air close to her cheek. She kisses me on the mouth.

"How are you?" she says.

"Fine." I unzip my jacket then seat myself on the sofa next to my mother's bundled feet. I am instantly sleepy.

"How am *I?*" she asks.

My brother lifts an eyebrow at me.

"How're you feeling?" I say.

"Awful."

"She feels awful," Grandma echoes.

"But do you like it?" I say. "Are you happy with it?"

"How can I be happy when I feel so awful?" Mom turns her head and pulls back her hair, deliberately revealing stitches winking out from inside and behind her ears like false eyelashes.

"Don't show me!—please." I add, "You know, after a man gets a facelift he has to shave behind his ears."

My brother throws back his big head and laughs. He has deep crow's-feet feathering his eyes.

"I put on makeup so you wouldn't be disgusted by me," she says through her teeth.

I turn to my brother. "How was your drive?"

"I had to keep slapping myself in the face to stay awake. Fourteen hours."

"They cut off nine inches of flesh," my mother says. "My scar is twenty-six inches across."

"Twenty-six inches," my grandmother repeats. "Can you imagine that?"

My mother pulls down her blankets, pulls her sweatpants down to her abdomen. There are no bandages. She's got yellowed plastic tubes protruding from each hip on either end of the tummy tuck gash, curving down like catfish whiskers. Even her navel has stitches.

Her belly is a cyclops catfish monster goggling at me with its black hairy eye.

"They had to make a new bellybutton 'cause the old one got cut off." Grandma is giddy; she looks a little stoned. "You," she says to my brother, "you keep an eye on her and make sure she doesn't eat everything in sight so she doesn't get fat again."

My mother reaches for the newspaper spread out on the coffee table, knocking over her bottle of Percodan. She picks up the funnies with both hands and begins chewing the pages, tearing off little pieces with her teeth and spitting them onto the carpet.

"What are you doing?" Grandma asks.

"I'm eating everything in sight." They both laugh. I spot a check peeking out from under the papers on the coffee table— Pay to the Order of the first three letters of my name in Grandma cursive. I look away quickly, secretly thrilling.

My brother goes down the hall to the bathroom. He opens the door and I get a noseful of peach potpourri.

"I'm starving," I say. Partly to get my mind off that money, for now. "What should we do for lunch?"

"We just had breakfast," says Grandma. "But you could fix yourself a snack. I'd love some potata chips. I haven't had potata chips in years."

"There's potato chips," Mom says.

"No, no, no. I love them but I can't eat them. I'll get fat."

My mother turns to me. "There's beef barley soup." She's rotating the little ball of cartilage on the end of her nose. It's a habit. She likes the cracking sound.

In the kitchen, I flip the switch and the fluorescent light shudders on.

The fridge is full of condiments mostly and soft drinks, tubs of leftovers. When I pull out the crisper, a head of iceberg rolls and bumps the front of the drawer. My brother comes in and reaches around me for a jug of diet cola.

I ask him if he got his check yet. He pats the back pocket of his jeans.

"You okay?"

"Yeah, I'm fine," he says.

"You don't look so good."

"Thanks a lot."

"He's sick." My mother humps into the kitchen. "What're your plans for Christmas?"

"What do you mean, sick?"

"He's in horrible pain every night. It's only at night. Are you coming up for Christmas?"

"No. I'm not." I start flinging open cupboard doors. One entire cabinet is stacked full of cups of instant minestrone. By multiplying height (five) times width (six) times guesstimated depth (six?) I figure there are at least a hundred and eighty soups. "So. What is it? What's wrong with him?" I ask my mother though my brother is right there.

"Ugh, too cold. Hurts my teeth." My brother sets the soda on the countertop and rubs his front teeth.

I touch him on the arm and say, "Do you know what's wrong with you?" He shrugs. I can't tell if this is his answer or if he wants me to take back my hand.

"Why can't you come for Christmas?" My mother plunks herself down at the table. Something thuds against the kitchen window, hard enough to rattle the glass.

"What the hell was that?" I say.

"Oh, that. It took me the longest time to figure out." She seems delighted. Beneath the kitchen light her bruises are more apparent, even behind the dark lenses, even under all that foundation makeup. "I'd be driving along in my car and I kept hearing this rolling sound above my head, whenever I pulled to a stop or started up again—this awful rolling sound."

"Hey, where is your car?" I break in. "There's a minivan in the driveway."

"I was wondering if you'd noticed. That's my new car."

"What happened to the old one? You just bought it. Like two years ago. Not even."

"It caught on fire," she deadpans. My brother's laughing at this. "I was on the freeway and I smelled smoke. I look back over my shoulder and there's all this black smoke! So I get off the freeway—you know the gas station right next to the Henny Penny Restaurant?—well I pulled into that gas station."

"Your car was on fire and you pulled into a gas station."

"Yes! I can only imagine what they all must've been thinking when they saw me coming straight for them! People came running out of the Henny Penny's with fire extinguishers so I just sat in the car and waited for them to put it out."

"You stayed in the car?"

"Well then these guys started saying, 'It's gonna blow! Get her out!' and I got out, but by that time there was so much smoke, I couldn't see a thing. And they couldn't see me—they were still yelling, 'Get her outta there!' and I had to scream, 'I'm out, I'm out!' So anyway I got a new car. I don't like it. Only gets twenty-one miles to the gallon. Do you keep track of your gas mileage?"

My brother says, "My car gets thirty-two. Sometimes thirty-six," and goes back into the living room with a box of Better Cheddars tucked under his arm.

"Wait." I press a fingertip to my ear, my ears are ringing. "What about the whateveritwas that just crashed into the window?"

"Yes! That rolling noise. Drove me nuts. Like something—like marbles sliding back and forth. Like the sound of a sliding glass door opening and closing. At first I thought maybe it was only in my head, but then I decided no, it was real. So I pried part of the ceiling off the car—couldn't find a thing. But then I looked up and saw that I was parked under the juniper, and the juniper was covered with berries. Sure enough, there were all these dried-up juniper berries caught in that little metal rim that goes between the doors and the roof of the car. Boy, was I glad to have solved that one. Anyway, there's these blue jays that keep hurling themselves at the window—like just now. First few times I thought they were trying to attack me. And they hit the window so hard sometimes they leave bloody smears. Weren't you going to get something to eat?"

"Ugh."

"Isn't it just awful? It really upsets me. But finally I figured out that all the birds have been eating juniper berries: they're getting drunk! They get drunk and attack their own reflections in the window. It's so upsetting! And it reminds me of when my father took me and my brother and sister out for ice cream. He must've thought the front door at the soda fountain was open but it wasn't—it was glass, maybe it had just been cleaned. Wham! There's this bloody face print on the door and his nose is bleeding all down his front. So Pop mops himself up with napkins and orders a strawberry milkshake. Now you really have to picture him, blood everywhere," she laughs. "He gets his milkshake and, and—"

She doubles over from laughing, palms clapped to the sides of her face like she's literally trying to keep her seams from splitting.

"He sticks his straw in and milkshake shoots up all over his face. He was just dripping with blood and pink milkshake. It was so awful, we couldn't stop laughing! And that's what the birds make me think of. So what is it you're doing for Christmas?" Then, before I can answer—"Well I'm not going to be here for Christmas. I'm going to Florida. Your brother too. Want to come?"

"You still haven't said what's wrong with him—do you know what's wrong?"

"He has a disease, we think." She puts a hand between her legs and squeezes her inner thigh. "A rare incurable disease. Yep, yep, yep."

All the phones in the house start beetling at once, raising the hairs on the back of my neck. It starts up again and breaks off mid-ring. "Oh, it's you," I hear Grandma say in the other room. "Well how are you? . . . good, good . . . yes, she is. Gorgeous."

"What kind of disease?" I ask.

"Pay-am," Grandma calls. "Pam!" My mother pulls herself up to field the call.

The bathroom affords some privacy but it is not a restful room. Too many mirrors. And evidently my mother's taken up trompe l'oeil. One pink wall is crawling with ivy, and above the toilet she's painted a picture of a shelf with a vase and flowers on it. The peach smell's coming from a real bowl on the counter filled with real dyed-orange wood shavings. While I pee, my cubist reflections eye me fatly from all sides. I fold the hanging square of toilet paper into a triangle, the way they do in hotels. I don't wash my hands in the faux-marbleized sink.

Everyone's back on the sofa. Grandma looks up and says, "Jim's coming over in about an hour." My stepfather, soon to be ex-stepfather.

"I want him to see how good I look," says my mother, gritting her teeth. Then, "Yikes! I'm leaking! Paper towels— quick!" My brother jumps up and goes fast into the kitchen. He comes back waving a long flag of paper towels. Mom snatches it and rips it in half. She makes two wads and shoves them under her waistband. To me she says, "Before I had these plastic baggy thingies attached to my tubes, but the doctor took them off on Tuesday. So now the fluid just drains out all over my pants."

I say softly, "I don't understand why you still see him."

"My doctor?"

"No. Jim."

She pauses. "I told him from now on he has to pay me a hundred dollars if he wants to have sex with me."

Grandma slowly shakes her head. "At least you had good sex," she says. "At least there was that. I think I'll have some of that soup." She gets up from the sofa.

"Guess I'll have a sandwich," says my brother, following her into the kitchen.

"There's meatloaf in the fridge," Mom points out. Then she leans close to me and whispers very loud, "She and my father never had good sex."

"Mom," I say before she goes further. "Don't talk to me about sex. Please."

"Did I tell you I bought your grandmother a vibrator?" she says. "She tells me she hasn't used it yet. Your check's on the coffee table."

I look at her like *check?* What is this word *check?*

She rifles through the mess of Sunday paper. "Right here." She picks up the little yellow slip and flaps it in the air in front of my face. A fan of blurry zeros. My brother comes back with a meatloaf sandwich and sits down between us.

"Oh!" Grandma whoops from the kitchen. "Delicious!"

"You like the soup?" my mother shouts.

"No, this peach ice cream! Oh! This is so good I could just throw up!"

I hear the microwave ding.

"So," I say to my brother. "You're really sick."

Mom says, "Whatever you do, don't tell him he's too skinny—he's extremely self-conscious. That looks good." Nods at my brother's sandwich. "Maybe I'll have one too." She lifts herself off the sofa and goes hunching toward the kitchen; she reaches the doorway at the precise moment Grandma appears, balancing her bowl of soup.

Their foreheads smack, and a wave of soup and twirling spoon goes up in midair, as I brace myself for the crush of crockery. Instead the bowl bounces once off the carpet, noiselessly, and rolls on its side, landing at my feet, wet side down.

"You guys okay?" I ask. My brother leaps up. I stay where I am.

I reach for the check and fold it into my pocket. I've known for several months that my grandma's lawyer advised her to give away a chunk of what Pop left her. Tax purposes. Pop's death is how my mother paid for her surgery. I uncap the Percodan, spill out a cupped palmful, and put this in my pocket too.

I give the soup bowl a kick to right it. I take it to the kitchen, stepping over my brother who's in the doorway sponging up soup from the carpet and the kitchen floor, mostly the carpet. Like mother and daughter monkeys, the two of them pick barley and threads of beef out of each other's hair, mostly my mother's hair. They're laughing. We all are. My brother laughs like *hyuk, hyuk, hyuk*.

Mom's glasses fall off her face and clatter onto the floor. Bruise-colored rivulets show on her cheeks where tears of laughter have made her makeup run. She gasps, clutching her abdomen. Then she crumples. It happens slow, like a crepe paper streamer, torn free, hanging in the air before it begins its flitting descent. She's trying to say something, I can't understand what at first because she's still laughing. "Burst," is what she's saying. "I've burst."

I let out with an involuntary broken cackle, like a hiccup.

"My stomach—"

"Call 911!" I cry.

"No!" Mom wails. "They'll send an ambulance. It's too expensive. I can't afford an ambulance!"

"We'll take the car," I say.

"Not my car," she insists, "not my new car. I'll ruin the seat covers."

"Okay, we'll take my car." My calm surprises me.

"No, we'll take your brother's car. He'll drive."

I am a little offended. She reaches under her waistband and fishes out a tube. The tip of it is gluey with blood.

Meantime, my brother disappears and comes back with sneakers and a clean sweatshirt for her. I get down on the floor with him, and we each lace up a shoe. Grandma's gone rummaging for a comb. From the living room, I hear a glassy thunk. I think, *Of course.* Of course there are drunk birds flying into the windows. I help my mother pull off her shirt, careful not to lift her arms too high, so she doesn't rip further. Me undressing her, this feels all wrong, backwards. I wet a paper towel with warm water and crouch over her, wiping soup from her face and neck, mindful of stitches hidden behind her ears.

Aunt Mae, the car, stutters into reverse. The original Aunt Mae lived to be a hundred and five. With money she got when Aunt Mae died, my mother bought a new used car and named it Aunt Mae, and now Aunt Mae is my brother's.

Mom doesn't look at her new face in the mirror or down at her stomach and think *Pop*, does she?

"Stop! Go back, I forgot my purse!" Mom says.

"I've got your purse right here," I say, rolling down the window to get some air.

She always keeps a cache of candy in her purse, in her underwear drawer too. Digging for candy, I find a Polaroid of my mother all bruised. From before the face-lift. From Jim. I pick out a lime lollipop.

"Jim's truck!" says my mother, shaking her fists like maracas. "That was Jim!"

Out the back window I see, sure enough, it is Jim's truck, slowing, then I am thrown forward as my brother brakes hard.

Jim gets down from the cab of his pickup and swaggers stiff-legged toward us. One leg is noticeably shorter than the other from his most recent car wreck. He sticks his head through my window, I turn my head sharply, and his kiss hits the side of my face. Jim says he's not coming to the hospital, he needs to pick up a few things at the house.

On the freeway, my mother says, "Jim's stealing from me."

"But the tools are his," says my brother.

"He didn't buy them, I did."

From sucking so hard on my lollipop, the roof of my mouth is scraped raw.

"Good thing you're on all those painkillers," says Grandma to my mother. "If you weren't on so many drugs already—"

"I'd be in agony." In the side-view mirror on the passenger door I see my mother's image, very small, pushing and rolling the fleshy ball of her nose.

The off-ramp wraps around a Little League field where I used to watch my brother pitch (*Rock and fire,* Jim would coach him, *rock and fire*). Now, the back fence of the playing field is crowded with figures uniformed in pale blue and yellow, all flocked to some commotion in the adjacent hospital lot. There are a dozen police cars at least, lights whirling and bouncing off the stucco walls of the medical complex, the Channel 7 News van is here too. We make a wide circle around the scene and pull up to the emergency entrance. My mother rejects my offer to run ahead and find her a wheelchair.

Inside the corridor there is no bustling activity, only us, only the quick rubbery squeak of our soles on the gold linoleum. My brother will meet up with us after he parks Aunt Mae. In the reception area, my mother marches up to the front window, slaps her hands flat on the countertop, and announces, "I'm having complications." The receptionist slides open the window, pushes a clipboard and pen at my mother, and I'm staring at long blue fingernails with yellow duckies painted on them, some wearing tiny sailor hats tipped jauntily. The glass snaps shut.

We fill out the forms. We wait. Aside from the lady with the amazing nails behind the window, and the talk show host whose face, so fraught with concern, looms from the TV bracketed to the wall, we three are the only bodies in the waiting room.

"He has such small hands," my mother murmurs.

"Who?" I ask.

"My doctor. Those hands, I knew he'd do a good job because he has such tiny little hands."

I say, "Well I don't think he did such a great job. You're coming apart."

"It's my own fault. I'm too fat. That's why I burst, I'm just too fat."

"You are not too fat." Searching for support, I look to Grandma, but she's looking up at the TV. "That's not why this happened. Your doctor didn't sew you up right is why."

Out of the sides of my eyes I see an old man come in. He says, "Somebody's been shot. Killed." I realize when I hear the voice that this old man is my younger brother.

A male nurse in scrubs pushes through the double doors with a wheelchair. After glancing at each of us, he moves toward my brother and takes him lightly by the elbow, guiding him to his seat. "No, no! Not him," we clamor. "Her!" Both the nurse and my brother blush. My mother is whisked away.

My brother sifts through the magazines, chooses one, and sits in the far corner of the room. He flips the pages very fast. Grandma nervously butters her slacks with her hands. A commercial comes on TV, a man's hand cupping a mound of peas. I jam my hands into my jacket pockets, feeling something in there. The pills. My check.

For a full minute I watch Grandma watching the talk

show's closing credits. A small moon of light shines off her bald spot, which is about the size of a quarter. Makes her look sort of holy. Monkish. "Grandma," I say. "I just want to tell you how much I appreciate the money."

"Thank your grandfather," she says. "You know I talk to him all the time. On the Ouija board. Last time I asked him, 'How're you doing Pop,' he told me, 'Dead.'" She leans toward me and extracts a little white feather from my hair. "I was cleaning out the attic and I found all these shirts of his. Still in their packages, never opened. It's so sad. He'll never wear them."

I wonder am I obligated to write a thank-you note now that I've thanked her in person?

"Good afternoon," says the TV newsman whose head is brick-shaped and -colored. "Top story we're working on for today: a prominent plastic surgeon slain. Dr. Barry Muske gunned down this morning in his office while his wife looked on. Police are looking for this suspect, a former patient—"

"Muske!" Grandma cries. "Oh my gravy, that's Pam's doctor!"

I feel oddly elated. Lightheaded.

"—hit list of doctors—"

God, I'm ravenous, I haven't eaten at all today. Just that sucker.

"—breast augmentation surgeries. Join the Channel 7 News family for those details, and more, at five."

I'll get something for each of us. Potato chips for Grandma. Somewhere there must be a snack machine.

The Good Life

SHE WROTE: *Daer Tooth Fairy, I lost my tooth. Love, Valerie.* She drew a heart and two stars on the note and put it with her tooth under the pillow. Now it is morning, but when she lifts the pillow, she finds her tooth and note still there.

Her mother comes in with Cheerios and hands the bowl up to Valerie in the top bunk. She climbs up a rung and touches her lips to Valerie's forehead. "Still warm," she says.

"Mother," says Valerie, who doesn't normally call her mother *Mother,* "you forgot about my tooth." Her mother hurries out down the hall.

The cereal bowl is large and heavy to hold, slippery with condensation. Valerie makes a table out of Alfred, the stuffed dog, who has no eyes and curly hair, real hair. With the quilt pulled over Alfred in her lap, she looks lumpily pregnant.

Her mother returns and feels around under Valerie's pillow. She says, "Maybe you didn't look hard enough—aha!" She pulls out a silver dollar, big as Valerie's palm.

When her mother was pregnant, Valerie knew it would be a baby brother, to make her family fair: two boys, two girls—father, mother, sister, brother, slanting tallest to littlest.

Last night her brother was in her dreams. Outside on the porch, she sat him on the railing, held him up by the armpits. The house is on a hill, built on stilts, so they were high above the devil down on the ground, a furry devil with the face of a boy about her age, like a boy in a bear suit with horns instead of ears. Stomp, stomp, went the devil, and the house shook so hard she lost hold of her brother, and the earth swallowed him and the devil both. So she went to Hell to kidnap him back. Hell was not all fire like she thought, it was satiny, with lots of cushions, a Valentine chocolate box. On a heart-shaped bed, her brother lay in the dimple he made, and she scooped him up, steadying his head with the crook of her arm. When the tassel of a silken rope brushed her cheek, she pulled it, and elevatored up to the top bunk.

All that's left in the cereal bowl now is milk.

She pops the scab off a bug bite on her cheek and sucks blood from her fingernail, which sets the mother in her head to scolding, Don't pick. Past the plastic horses that stand on her windowsill, the red shale cliff of Red Hill blazes in the early sun. Below it, in the shopping center, she can make out the tiles of letters that spell Safeway.

Red Hill is a good name for Red Hill, Valerie thinks. Her hill is Mount Baldy, because on top there's a patch where no trees grow.

The boulevard glitters with ant cars. Over there, that black spot is the blacktop of her elementary school, empty today, Saturday.

Today, like yesterday, Valerie has a fever and can't go out and play.

"Mom," she calls. "Mom! Mom! Mom!"

From the doorway, her mother says, "Shush!—your *father*."

He is always sleeping. He snores and shakes, kicks in his sleep, and lately her mother's been sleeping in Valerie's room, in the bottom bunk, the bed reserved for the baby when he's big enough.

At the same hospital where Valerie and her brother were born, her father had surgery to have a cow's vein grafted inside his wrist. A dialysis needle, thick as a drinking straw, will collapse an ordinary human vein.

"What?" her mother says. "What now?"

Valerie mimes drinking from a huge cup.

Since her father's kidneys failed, he can't pee. During dialysis, which is the only time he can drink, he drinks ginger ale.

When her mother comes back with a plastic glass of grape juice and orange aspirin, Valerie's sprawled on the carpet, surveying the camping trip in miniature she created yesterday. The blankets are potholders she made at school out of old tights. Ken and Barbie are *man* and *woman*, not Mom and Dad. Having a camper van is the good life.

Her mother huffs at the cereal bowl nestled in the sheets and takes it away.

Today the Barbies will go horseback riding. They will ride horses to the top of Red Hill. Valerie's tongue keeps going back to the hole where her tooth was, to the chip of new tooth already coming in. She chews the aspirin. Tastes like candy, tangy and sweet. She drinks her juice and vomits.

Purple! Valerie is stunned by the violence of it, the suddenness and the color, and so many unchewed O's.

Valerie gets out of her nightgown, wads it up, and puts it in with the dirty clothes in the hall closet. Her mother's in the living room, rocking the baby in his bouncy chair with her foot while she crochets. Naked except for underpants, Valerie waits outside the bathroom for someone who's peeing—not her father, he can't pee—to come out. This loud stream seems to never end. Valerie's face in the doorknob is all nose. The sound stops and starts again, then finally stops. The door opens and it's Jimmy who lives a couple houses up the road. He lives in the garage.

Jimmy comes over to help. He put together the bunk bed. Saturdays he does yardwork and sometimes he babysits. He's nineteen, a big kid. On his t-shirt, a skeleton wears a crown of roses. He makes the whistle of the Intercontinental Ballistic Tickle Missile, arcing his finger toward Valerie's ribs. She shrieks, and he launches another attack. Her mother shushes and shakes her crochet hook at them, and then the bedroom door opens. They've waked her father.

He is so thin. Rainbow suspenders keep his pants from falling down.

Last year, Mrs. Sours said, "Who's that man with the rainbow suspenders?" Mrs. Sours was Valerie's kindergarten teacher. "I've seen you walking with him. Is that your grandfather?"

"No. My dad." On days he wasn't doing dialysis, they went for a walk. If Valerie said she was too tired from the uphill walk home from school, he told her to stop whining. Sometimes she hid. Now, the walks are shorter, slower, he is winding down.

Mrs. Sours said, "Your father, is he very old?"

"He's sick."

After that, Mrs. Sours invited the family over for tea. Valerie's father stayed home and slept. Her mother, who was very pregnant at the time, couldn't get enough scones, and though she's not fond of hot drinks, she drank tea to be polite. Valerie had fruit punch. In the other room, where the walls were green with a white design, a flowering design not unlike what Valerie sees inside her eyelids, Mr. Sours sat on the orange couch, watching television. Valerie took the doily off the couch's arm and draped it on her head. "Are you pregnant?" she asked Mr. Sours, referring to his beach ball stomach. He cupped his hand beside his eye, making a small wall between himself and Valerie. "You're old," she said. "You're going to die soon."

In the car on the way home, her mother said, "None of their plants were real."

Just to get from the bedroom to the bathroom, Valerie's father needs to use a cane, and soon he will need two, two four-pronged canes. And then he will crawl. Her father gets to use the bathroom first—he's sickest, and he is the father after all.

If Valerie were the one dying, she'd be brushing her teeth by now. If she were dying, she'd be at Disneyland. "Mama," she says, which is what she used to say. "Mama, I threw up."

Fever broken, Valerie's feeling much better, she's silly and electric, playing Hot Lava at her great-great Aunt Mae's. She cheats, using cushions on the floor as stepping-stones to get from mohair sofa to lion-footed throne chair, then from there it's easy—chair to marbletop coffee table, this is an ice floe, to ottoman, and so on. Aunt Mae doesn't care, she just sits in her wheelchair, sort of bobbing her head. She's ninety-two. She doesn't have all her marbles. The nurse doesn't care. The nurse is concerned about Valerie's mother counting the silver. Valerie's mother cares about the silver.

For lunch, they go to Shakey's Pizza, Aunt Mae's treat. When Valerie's mother yells out the available toppings, Aunt Mae nods yes at mushrooms and pepperoni, so that's what they get, though she is always nodding. She nods spastically. Valerie's mother has salad bar.

For the millionth time, Valerie says, "Valerie." She says, "I'm six." She says, "147 Peerless Avenue. Please pass me a piece with not a lot of mushrooms on it. Aunt Mae? Can I please have another piece of pizza, please?"

"What was your name, dear?"

"Valerie."

"How old are you, Valerie?"

"Six. I said I was six."

"Where do you live?"

"147 Peerless Avenue."

"And what's your name?"

Louder, "Valerie."

"That's a nice name, Valerie. What's your name?" Then she says, "If a person had a delicate stomach, pizza might be a very bad thing to eat." The baby spikes his gummed crust at the floor.

"Aunt Mae?" Valerie's mother tears off a new crust. "Are you feeling all right?"

After dropping Aunt Mae off, they stop at Red Hill Shopping Center to run errands. At Safeway, Valerie's a little mother, pushing her brother in his stroller while her mother pushes the cart. Her mother has a clicker to keep track of how much food stamp money she's spent. Next, they go over to Long's to fill her father's prescriptions. Valerie asks if she and the baby can stay in the toy section. In her coat pocket, the silver dollar is hot from her fingering.

Jacks and jump ropes. Play-Doh. Parachute guys. Cap guns, water pistols, ray guns that light up and shoot sparks. Her father does not allow guns. Valerie aims a ray gun at her brother, shooting blue sparks. A toy doctor set comes with a stethoscope, a first-aid kit, and a not-sharp syringe. Pull back the plunger and it fills up with fake blood.

Here's a machine that turns ordinary paper into money. Magic. Straw into gold. It costs ninety-nine cents.

Her mother is taking a long time, longer than prescriptions usually take, so Valerie puts the money maker in the stroller's pouch and wheels her brother toward the pharmacy. Her mother's not there. Valerie returns to the toy section—no mother. From weaving up and down the aisles, Valerie is sweaty and limp. No mother anywhere. There she is, looking at toothbrushes. "Mom!" Valerie says. Her mother looks up, and it is not her.

Their car was parked by the bears. Not real bears, smooth granite bears. The car isn't there.

The baby throws his pacifier into the bears' bed of wood-chips. He makes no sound when he cries, just tears. Valerie tells him, "Don't misbehave." She wipes splinters off the paci-fier and sticks it back in his mouth. Then she pulls herself up onto a bear, pressing her cheek to its cool hump. She hears a faint humming. The hum makes her sleepy.

"What a pretty baby girl."

Valerie opens her eyes. An old man is bent over her brother, a large man with large ears and large lips, stomach stuck out like a beach ball. It's Mr. Sours, the old man from the tea party last year, before her brother was born. "He's not a girl," Valerie says, "he's a boy."

Mr. Sours' nose is some unusual fruit. He says, "Is he your son?"

"No. My brother."

"Can I take him for a walk?"

"Okay."

The last sunlight flares through Red Hill's fringe of eucalyptus.

Red Hill is dark. In its shadow, Valerie hugs the cold flanks of her bear, riding through an enchanted wood, all silver trees and windchime leaves. Far away, someone is calling her name. Someone is saying, "Oh my God, thank you, thank you, God! I got halfway home before I remembered—"

"You forgot us." Valerie slides off the bear and lands in a heap in the woodchips because her legs are asleep.

"Where is your brother?"

"With Mr. Sours."

"Who—?"

"Mr. *Sours.*" Yanked to her feet, pulled along by the arm, Valerie's running on pins-and-needles to keep up, as her white-faced mother marches toward Safeway.

"Mr. Sours," her mother says, "is dead."

All you can do now is wait, that's what the police say. Go home. Dinner is reheated pizza. Only Valerie and her father eat. Her mother cleans—she wipes, she scours, she vacuums and sweeps, and with the broom she stabs at daddy longlegs up in the corners, brushes away their webs. Valerie picks mushrooms off her pizza and drops them onto the floor. Her father's jaw makes popping noises as he chews, and the pulsing of his cow vein shivers the chain of his Medic Alert bracelet.

Waiting feels like bees and ants, same as when her brother was born, waiting for him to come home from the hospital. Jimmy babysat that night and gave Valerie her bath. He twisted her hair into soapy horns and cut up carrots for Valerie stew.

Valerie sneezes. Her father's napkin whooshes off the table, and when he bends to pick it up, he points at the oily pile under her chair. "What is this?"

"Mushrooms."

Clean that up and go to your room is what she expects him to say. "Clean that up," he says, "and get your coat on." They're going for an evening walk.

"I don't feel so good," says Valerie, pulling her legs up out of the broom's way.

Her mother says, "You're going?"

"To get some air," her father says.

Her mother throws the broom down, bang on the floor, and slides open the window over the kitchen sink. "There," she says. "Air."

Her father says, "Tell your mother you're sorry."

"I'm sorry."

"Sorry for what," he says.

She is sorry for hating walks with her father. Sorry she gave away her brother. She says, "I'm sorry for dropping mushrooms on the floor."

Stairs rise from the house to the road, where an insect cyclone whirrs in the cone of greenish streetlight. Her father puts his cane up a step and lifts a foot, like moving underwater, wrongly slow, then the other foot, up twenty steps. At the top, Valerie bursts into a skip. He tells her, "You wait."

She waits, and when he catches up, she babysteps.

"So," he says. "How was school?"

"Today's Saturday." She claps at a mosquito.

"How was school yesterday?"

"Yesterday I was sick and my tooth fell out." Touching the silver dollar in her pocket, she remembers the toy she put in the stroller's pouch. That money maker, she never paid for it. She stole. She left Long's without paying. She forgot.

"Look," her father says. "You can see the Milky Way." All she sees is a smear of stars. Then, headlights. Brights flashing, horn blaring. Valerie and her father huddle in the glare. She holds on to the thin bar of his arm.

Her mother shouts, "Get in, get in!"

They found her brother.

Valerie can't sleep. She's thinking about digging a hole. She'll take the money maker outside, under the porch, and dig a hole for it. She'll whisper things into the hole, like wishing her father would hurry up and die, or that she sometimes presses on her brother's soft spot, and she'll cover the toy and what she's whispered with dirt.

The bottom bunk is empty. In the grainy light, she finds the money maker and closes it back into its box. It doesn't really turn paper into money, it's just a trick.

Tiny red shoes sit on the kitchen counter. The police went door to door and found the baby at The Embers, a bar just two doors down from Safeway. The drunk man had bought him shoes.

Valerie sets the money maker next to the shoes. She gets on a chair to reach the sink and puts her mouth on the faucet, drinking until it would hurt to drink more. She smells smoke. Out the window, she sees her mother and Jimmy on the porch, moonlit, sharing a cigarette. Her mother's shoulders shake, and Jimmy keeps kissing the top of her hair.

Valerie goes back to bed and sucks the silver dollar.

At Sunday breakfast, there they are, front page, full color: father wearing rainbow suspenders, mother looking some-where off to the side, Valerie with her eyes closed, and her brother in his new red shoes.

TWO

Big Guy

"HAVE YOU EVER," says Andy. He sits in the easy chair and plucks at a tuft of chair stuffing that pushes through a burn on the arm. The chair is the only furniture in Emmett's apartment. The table is the floor. The bed is the floor. Emmett sits cross-legged on carpet the color and texture of scrambled egg.

"Ever what?" says Emmett.

"Never mind."

"Ever what?"

"*Done* one." They work at the hospital, orderlies both. Andy transports items. Item means food tray and item also means dead body. Emmett mops up down in Pathology.

"I think I know what you're asking," says Emmett.

"There're rumors."

Emmett tears a curl of label off the tequila bottle, rolls it tight, flicks it at Andy. "I ain't done nothing, no sir," says Emmett. "You?"

"Of course not. But one time this item comes in, boy no more than fifteen maybe sixteen. So damn sad. He was *perfect*. Lips still red, like he was only sleeping, like Snow White, and his mouth made me think—"

"You can't stick it in the mouths. 'Less you want it bit off."

"No, no," says Andy. "I just wanted to kiss him."

"Kiss." Emmett rubs the bluish tattoo gone awry on his forearm. Exhales loudly.

Andy stands up. The floor wavers and woozes. He pauses to steady himself, then heads for the bathroom. Shuts himself in with the stink and unzips his coveralls. He prefers coveralls because they have no waistband. He buys them secondhand. He wrests his arms out of the sleeves, flinging his cigarettes, Bic, and inhaler out of the breast pocket embroidered with the name Roy. His things skitter across the flooring under the sink.

Andy lowers himself to pick up his things, then comes up too fast, bongs his head against the sink's porcelain lip. He pats the spot where his hair is beginning to thin, feeling for blood. Tender but dry.

On a skinny shelf hung above the sink, eight or nine black-capped vials stand single file. Pathologist's vials. Andy sits to pee, his belly blousing onto his lap, and leans in for a closer look at the row of bottles. Hair. Dark hair, plus one red and two blond. "What's all this hair?"

"My collection," Emmett says through the door.

"You collect hair?"

"Snatch."

Andy doesn't ask from where. He zips up and opens the door. Hooks his fingertips onto the top of the doorframe and does a deep knee bend, stretching. "I collect stuff too," he says. "Books. First editions mainly. Though Beckett, any edition of Beckett's worth something, even paperback."

"What's beckett?"

"Samuel Beckett the writer. You know, *Waiting for Godot.* Oh, and dolls."

"Dolls? You collect dolls?"

"Puppets," says Andy. "Ventriloquist dolls."

"Dummies you mean."

"I prefer dolls."

"Aww, scared of hurting their feelings?"

"No, I just take this very seriously. Like people who read science fiction, they don't say sci-fi. They say ess-eff."

"What's wrong with saying sci-fi?"

"It's—oh fuck me, I don't know. Anyway, I don't know why I said I collect dolls. I've only got two, a Charlie McCarthy and a Howdy Doody. How many of something do you have to have for it to be a collection?"

"Three probably."

"My mother collects cuckoo clocks and cookie jars," says Andy. "She had special shelves custom made." He leans against the doorframe and slides into a crouch.

Emmett strokes the tequila bottle's neck suggestively.

Andy pretends not to notice. He says, "When I visit my mother, I always bring her a new cookie jar. I love my mother, just love her to death. Mom's got no toes."

"I was born with extra pinkies," says Emmett, holding up his hands to show the scars. The nails on his remaining fingers are long for a man.

"She wasn't born that way," says Andy. "It's because of her arthritis—her *arthur-itis*. Doctor was supposed to replace the bones in her toes with plastic. The bandages come off and there's no toes. Just these, like, foot paddles with dimples on the ends. He cut her toe bones out and sewed her up without putting the plastic ones in. He forgot. How do you forget a thing like that?"

"Oh, but she's living high on the hog now."

"No, she thinks suing and lawyers are against God. She's stuck in a wheelchair. Before she could at least walk. Worst thing of it is, she's in pain still—she gets phantom pains. Sue the fucking sawbones? *No, it's God's will.* Same goes for why she never divorced my dad—*God's will.* Now give me that tequila. You feel like ordering a pizza?"

Andy worries. About his mother mostly. He also worries that the blood in his shit lately means he has cancer, like his father. Andy's consolation is that if he got cancer maybe he'd lose weight.

Emmett stands up, tugs open his button fly and says, "Pizza? Nah. I don't like pizza. Don't eat what I can't drink."

Andy is somehow unsurprised.

"I like V8 and Clamato and I like milk," says Emmett. "Tell you what I feel like is a shower."

"You look like a shower." What Andy thinks he looks like really is a slitty-eyed dun rat.

"There's Clamato in the fridge."

Andy pulls a sour face. "I don't do fish. Or mollusk for that matter."

Listening to the purr of running water, Andy sits in the chair and smokes, blowing smoke out his nose. In the shower, Emmett sings, "I love little baby ducks, old pickup trucks, slow- moving trains, and rain."

A song Andy's dad sang.

Andy considers bolting, but as soon as he thinks it, he feels a spasm in his chest, the air squeezing out. He can't go home. He taps ashes onto the carpet.

Today after lunch (a box of chocolate-covered donut holes) Andy was paged down to Pathology, where all hands were needed to hoist an especially cumbersome item. Andy, Emmett, and a pair of Bible College boys on work-study rolled the fat man off a lowered gurney that wouldn't pop up, he was too heavy, and beached him onto a sheet. On the count of three,

they all lifted and got him airborne but not quite high enough.
So they tried to bring him back down gently, gently. He was
dropped. First came a *crick-crick* thin ice sound, then the yel-
lowy splash.

When they were scrubbing together afterwards, Emmett
said to Andy, *I'd like to see you outside the hospital sometime.* And
Andy said they could go for a smoke right now. *No,* said
Emmett, *I mean you and me go out.*

Andy, caught off-guard, said without meaning to, *Sure, sure.*
"And I," Emmett croons from the shower, "love you too."

After the fat man debacle, Andy went up to Obstetrics to
watch the newborns being washed. At a double sink like any
kitchen sink, goopy babies are rinsed like dishes.

Andy hears the shriek of the tap shutting off. Emmett says,
"Get me a towel, will you. I'm dripping wet."

"Where's there a towel?"

"In my room someplace."

Andy finds a purple towel in a nest of socks and t-shirts,
used tissues, and sleeping bag. He cracks the bathroom door.
Emmett pulls the door open all the way, spilling out steam and
ammonia dank. He takes the towel and drops it on the floor.
"Get down," he says, "on your knees, big guy." Andy does
what he is told. Emmett comes into the living room and steps
up to Andy. He swivels his hips slow, slapping Andy's cheeks
with his soft drunk dick.

"My dad died last night," says Andy, who has no idea why
he said it now. Saying it out loud, saying it to someone else, is
like poking his tongue into the raw hole where a tooth was. He
hadn't intended to tell anybody because he feared he'd be
treated with too much courtesy, as if he would break, and the
idea of anyone treating him that way made him feel lonely and
phony.

"Little orphan Andy," says Emmett, neither kind nor unkind. "So you want to fuck? You want me to fuck you." He pulls the hoop of Andy's zipper, opening his coveralls down to his stomach. Andy sucks in and gets a bumpy feeling in his skin. He wishes he'd worn an undershirt. He can't bear being naked. Being in his body is unbearable.

"Turn out the light," he says. "Please?"

Emmett turns out the living room and bathroom lights. Then he comes up behind Andy and slides the coveralls off his shoulders, tumbling cigs, lighter, inhaler out from the breast pocket that says Roy. Andy's skin fuzzes into grainy particolor molecules as Emmett's eyes adjust. In the dark, Emmett can't see silver stretchmarks tigerstriping Andy's hips and breasts. Can't see the hairless rings around Andy's areolas, hairless and gummed with linty pills of adhesive from tape Andy uses sometimes, like he's done since he was twelve, to flatten the girlish puffiness of his nipples. Emmett pushes Andy forward onto all fours. "What'd he do?" says Emmett.

"Who do?"

"Your dad, what'd he do? For a living."

"Engineer."

"He drove a train?" Emmett pushes Andy's coveralls over his ass down to the crooks of his knees.

"No, Department of Public Works. He was in charge of regulating toxicity levels in the drinking water. Probably the water's what gave him cancer."

Emmett spreads Andy's asscheeks and pops his finger into the pucker just to the first knuckle. "Everybody gets cancer," says Emmett, "if something else don't get them first. Hold still."

Sickness had made Andy's dad a different person. This new father had said, *The clock struck one and you were born and zing-went-the-strings of my heart.*

.

Emmett wiggles his finger. Andy feels like he's got a lively peanut up his ass. With his other hand Emmett smacks him then soothes the smarting in circles with his palm. Smacks again harder and plunges inside and there is resistance. Again he plunges in and Andy, bayoneted by a fingernail, goes *mmph*. Bloom of stinging wet warmth and Emmett's finger slicks back and forth easy and faster.

Andy's father had said he was sorry, that discipline was the only way he knew how to be Dad. In Andy's breast a tuning fork had hummed. *I saw how much pain you were in, and I couldn't do anything because I was in so much pain myself.*

Emmett adds two more fingers.

Andy's nose tunes in to the rising odor of himself, swampy, sweetish, like water in which cut flowers have died. Then, like the great and powerful Oz, the face of his father lights up and hovers before him and Andy puts his hand on the wall, and now his dad is on the back of his hand. Andy pushes the wall to push away his father's face, to push himself out of his skin, filling himself with just fist so there's nothing left inside.

"Dude, you smell," says Emmett. "Peeyew. You smell rank."

On the phone this morning before sunup, when Andy's mother told him the news, her voice rose like the fact of his father's death was a question. Cancer wasn't what took him. Andy's mother woke because of the smell. She found him slumped over the heater, broiling. His heart stopped and that was where he fell. Father over easy.

Since he was little, Andy had wished his dad would hurry up and die, and now the wish has come true, but Andy doesn't feel like singing "Ding Dong, the Witch Is Dead!" after all. His own smell plugs his throat and he gags.

After the phone call, before his morning jog, Andy wrapped himself in Saran. Wearing just a jockstrap, he stood in the kitchenette and tightly wound plastic wrap around the tops of his thighs, his trunk, and upper arms, wishing himself smaller. Where he wraps regularly, his skin smells footy and tends to slough off. Then he ran. He smoked while he ran, puffed on his inhaler, puffed on his inhaler, puffed on his inhaler, hyper-aware of the hyper-sameness of everything. Too blue sky. Breaking sunlight too bright. He resented the intensity of green: too alive. Andy was too alive. Wheezing, but alive.

Hand pressed to the wall, his face bursting hot, blown up, Andy pushes to erase a photograph taken of him at twelve in his swimshorts on the banks of Clear Lake. Lips pulled back in a miserable show of teeth. Wide W of puppyfat titties. Same day he'd informed his dad at sunrise that he wasn't going fishing anymore ever—he couldn't kill what he wouldn't eat. The fishing poles came flying at his head, then the tackle box. Long ago, Andy unstuck this picture from the album and burned it.

His sweaty hand slips a little on the wall, bearing down to get Emmett's hand to fill him up till he splits.

Andy had raised his fist to his father once, and regretted it instantly, but he knew his father would be angrier if he backed down. So he drove his hand home toward his dad's chest, but his dad caught him by the wrist in midair. He dug his fingers into Andy's wrist, and Andy held his breath and bit his cheeks to keep from crying out. *Good,* his dad had said finally and released him.

A large bird flaps inside Andy's ribcage. *Whump, whump, whump.*

"Cuh, cuhh—"

Wings in his chest beat his breath away.

"—can't—"

Andy lets go of the wall and pats the fabric of his coveralls, bunching it, to feel for his inhaler which isn't there. Sweeps the floor with his arm. Emmett grinds his groin into Andy's hip.

"—breathe."

His fingers find the lighter first, then the inhaler. He gets it to his lips and pumps three puffs. Then he coughs and coughs and pulls away from Emmett with a suck sound. Crawls on his elbows into the bathroom, coughing as if he would heave his stubborn heart. He throws up a puddle of phlegm. The light clicks on in the living room.

"Fagotty Andy," says Emmett, "you bled on the rug."

"Meat tenderizer," Andy says in a feathery voice. "Make a paste of meat tenderizer. Dab it, don't rub. That'll take the spot right out."

"I don't eat meat, so what am I going to have meat tenderizer for?"

Andy croaks, "What do you want me to do? What do you want me to do about it, jackass?"

"Cool down, big guy. Forget it. Dude, you are so—*sensitive.*"

A breeze blows the trees, and orange streetlamps flicker through the leaves. Chill air rasps Andy's lungs. He pulls a cigarette from his pocket and lights it. When he gets home he'll call Domino's, whose pizza he hates but they're open late, if it's not too late. "You have the time?" he asks a tan man who stands with a poodle shaved like topiary, all pompoms, on a square of lawn.

"Eleven-oh-eight."

Andy notices a length of wrinkled white tape on the tan guy's forearm. "Sir, you have a piece of tape stuck to your arm."

"Skin cancer." Tan man smiles.

Andy walks on, weaving a little in his drunkenness. He

draws deeply from his cigarette, tingling in his head and fingertips. To keep warm, he breaks into sort of a skip. Hop-limp-jog, hop-limp-jog, it hurts between his legs.

Tonight he will eat a pizza, try to sleep, get up for work. The funeral is Wednesday, day after tomorrow. Tomorrow after work Andy will shop for a cookie jar for his mother, or maybe he won't go to work. Maybe he won't go to work ever again and Emmett will just disappear.

On a telephone pole up ahead is a sign that says LOST GOLDEN WHATEVER. Though when Andy gets closer he realizes he read it wrong, it says RETRIEVER not WHATEVER. He flicks his cig, aiming for the gutter, and it spins cockeyed into a hedge.

When he rounds his street corner he sees red lights flashing. A kid on a Big Wheel, Stephen from upstairs, comes pedaling down the sidewalk and skids to a stop. Stephen's toes bust through the too small feet of his pajamas.

"Hey, big guy," says Andy. "You're up late."

Stephen says, very vampish, "Call me Lola." Then he turns and rides back to the red lights. The lights are mounted on top of two fire trucks parked in front of Andy's building. His neighbors are all huddled birdlike in donated blankets on the grass across the street. Andy sees his house as a huge ghost face, like a child's drawing of a ghost. Firemen drag a soggy black sofa out of its mouth and litter the yard with char tossed down from the eyes.

"You live here, son?" says a fireman, swaggering up to Andy. "Roy? You live in number 2?"

"Yes."

"You have some kind of dolls?"

"Yes. Dolls."

The fireman lets out a poof of air. "Your dolls, they were on the heating unit."

"But I never turn on the heat, I don't even know how."

"Thermostat was set pretty high."

"Thermostat? I didn't know I had a thermostat."

"Whole building's on a thermostat. You got central heating."

"Captain Nichols," Andy squints at the fireman's nametag. "How do you know my room was where it started? Don't there have to be some forensics?"

"No, most times you can tell right away. Fire burns deeper at the source. Burn pattern's deepest around those dolls."

Andy feels a terrible desire to be enfolded in the fireman's coat and pound on his chest: *Hold me, Captain Nichols. Hold me!* Captain Nichols smells like wet smoke and rubber. Andy wipes his eyes and nose with his sleeve. Red lights sweep over him, over and over. "Stupid," he sobs. "Stupid, stupid."

Solo in the Spotlight

MOTHER crocheted and John the Gambler, he whittled. Animals mostly, potbellied old men, lined up single file on the mantel. When he wasn't whittling, he flipped the pages of catalogues that came to the house—Sears & Roebuck, ladies' clothing, Mother's magazines of yarn and crochet designs. John the Gambler wore a pair of crocheted slippers with rosettes on the toes. I, naturally, had no use for slippers.

John the Gambler was Mother's friend. He lived with us the summer I was eight. She called him John all that summer, and when he was gone he became John the Gambler.

This was back when I was collecting mermaids. I hadn't intended on collecting them. I saw one I liked, a china figurine, then Mother bought me another, and Mother's friend before John the Gambler added another. Three little mermaids on my vanity. I soon amassed a school of mermaids. This is what happens when people see that you have two or three of something.

On some nights, Mother put Arthur Murray on the hi-fi and practiced the cha-cha with John the Gambler. I watched and wished. Her sassy kicks, the click and scrape of her heels on the living room linoleum, made me wish I could give up my tongue for a set of legs, like the mermaid in the fairy tale. Though that one doesn't get the prince in the end. I did, I got mine, legs or no.

Days while Mother worked, John the Gambler took me to the Boardwalk. He liked the shows, he liked the rides. I think he liked me okay too. On account of my chair, we got to go right to the front of every line. He always smoked a little grass before we headed in; I didn't mind, and I didn't tell. Some days we'd go to the track, just the two of us. I liked to watch the horses run. I liked eating chocolate ice milk that John the Gambler fed to me from a wooden spoon.

SEE THE REAL MERMAID! is what the sign said at Neptune's Kingdom.

I was excited and breathing hard, and John the Gambler couldn't wheel me fast enough through the crowd. At the tank, people jumped aside, pulling their small children away from me by the shoulders. Don't stare, they mouthed. The mermaid was not a mermaid at all, it was a manatee, a sea cow. The placard above the tank said that sailors delirious with fever and starvation would see the manatees and hallucinate beautiful women. Mermaids. Many sailors leapt to watery graves chasing after manatees, apparently. I was crushed. I thought, I am a real mermaid. A fat brown beady-eye sea cow, that's me.

That evening, John the Gambler whittled me a manatee. He didn't mean to be unkind.

Another night he brought home a TV set. For two weeks, before he had to return it, Mother crocheted, John the Gambler whittled the Seven Dwarves, and I watched television. During the Mickey Mouse Club, they showed a commercial for a new doll, three of them on a stage, turning slow and shining under the lights like cars on a showroom floor. I want her, I said.

You have dolls already, said Mother. John the Gambler hollowed out Dopey's ear with his Swiss army knife.

It was true, I did have dolls, baby dolls. They didn't have fur-trimmed capes slung over evening gowns, bubble hairdos, mean sidelong eyes. They didn't have breasts.

The TV went away, and, for a time, John the Gambler was glum. I didn't care so much about the TV set, I only wanted that doll. Then, on one of his up days, John the Gambler took me to a toy store, said I could have anything I wanted. I picked the one in a black sparkly dress, strapless and molded to her body with a netting flounce at the ankles. Solo in the Spotlight, she was called. In her dress she looked like the pretty kind of mermaid, not the real kind.

When Mother saw it, she looked pained, and all the blood went out of her face like it did the time I asked her to paint my toenails (I've got *toes,* just not feet exactly). Oh for God's sake, said John the Gambler, slapping his thigh with a catalogue folded in half.

Eventually the sparkles wore off the front of the dress where my doll's chest stuck out.

John the Gambler went away, and Mother slid his carved figures off the mantel into a cardboard box. That manatee he made for me, I didn't keep it with the rest of my mermaid collection. I kept it on my nightstand where I could reach it with my head. I chewed it at night before falling asleep. My teeth loved the soft wood. When I asked Mother if I could have that box full of wood, she sighed, drew her lower lip in and let it go.

I still do it, collect odd wooden figures and chew them. I gnaw off the faces and limbs. Joe, my husband, he said what I do is art, so I became an artist. We're all some kind of artist: Mother crocheted, John the Gambler whittled, and Joe's art is fixing toasters. He put a motor on my chair, rigged it with a stick so I can drive it with my teeth. My *chair*iot. I get around on my own now, I do my sculptures, and I play music. With my tongue, of course. On the Boardwalk come summertime, me with my red-glitter electric keyboard, I'm practically famous.

The Monkey's Paw

UP CLOSE the sea foam is yellow and very dirty. Pretty, thinks
Mary, like an oil slick on a puddle of muddy rainwater is
pretty. She thinks of mermaids. Mermaids become sea foam
when they die. The only way a mermaid may attain an undy-
ing soul is to marry a mortal man and bear his child. "That's a
very patriarchal way of looking at it," says Mary to no one,
scuttling back as a wave slaps at her boots.

Lillian is farther up the beach looking for crab shells and
sand dollars, maybe a bleached-out bird skull if she's lucky.
Lillian, who sometimes doesn't come home—who knows
where she goes at night lately?—shrieks. Mary squints at her
through the thickening fog. Lillian's wedding veil sails out
behind her, snapping in the wind. There's a dark mound at Lillian's feet, not seaweed, something more solid than that.

"What is it?" Mary calls. She pulls off her glasses and licks
salt from the lenses to see better.

Before the beach, at work at the bookstore, Mary sat on a
stepstool on the mezzanine, alphabetizing Used Fiction to kill
time toward the end of her shift. She got as far as the G's,

retrieving errant García Márquezes from the M's, when she heard someone creeping up behind her. She tensed and turned, and there was Lillian, towering proudly, wearing a wedding veil over her cranberry-colored spiky hair. She was also wearing jodhpurs, and she held up a red globe formed of plastic squiggles, like cake-decorating gel hardened into a huge ball.

"What is it?" said Mary.

"A light," said Lillian, looking like a Statue of Liberty. "For the living room."

At this, a small pan warmed in Mary's chest.

In the car on the way to the beach, she chattered about Anton LaVey, the Black Pope of the Church of Satan, who was a regular customer at the bookstore. Today the Black Pope, in all black, of course, and a grandfatherish fisherman's cap, came up to Mary, who was reading *Women Who Kill*, though she was never supposed to read at the register, and he said, "Pardon me, can you tell me where True Crime has moved to?" She bent a page corner to mark her place. He said, "Do you always dog-ear your books?"

All day, *Do you always dog-ear your books?* played in Mary's head, and it plays now, as she marches through the dunes, against the sand-stinging wind, toward Lillian. More and more the mound becomes the shape of something dead. Coming closer she sees that it certainly is a dead body, and not whole. No arms, no legs, just a torso and a head. Instead of eyes, two pools of sand jittering with sand fleas brim its sockets. More fleas pop out of the matted black hair on its face and what's left of its body. Too much hair, Mary decides.

"It's an ape!" she cries.

Lillian nods.

"Well, well," says Mary. "What's it doing *here*?"

Lillian doesn't answer. Mary doesn't really expect her to.

They stand there awhile, as fog sponges up the remains of daylight.

A gust lifts Lillian's veil, snatching it from her head, and Mary chases as it blows toward the orange lights of the parking lot. She catches it, then something in the sand catches her eye. The hand. She whisks it up to show Lillian. Hairy and hard as a coconut, the hand is severed at the wrist, cleanly, not broken or chewed, and except for the thumb and pointer, all the other fingers have been chopped off at the knuckle.

They stop at the supermarket that used to be Playland-by-the-Sea for wine and Kitty Stew. In the pet food aisle, Mary drops to her knees and says to Lillian, "Marry me."

"Get up," says Lillian, tossing her veil as if it were long, long hair. "Get up," she says.

"Say yes."

Lillian yawns.

At home, Lillian is barefoot on the glasstop coffee table cut in the shape of a bone, stripping wiring once attached to a brass and woodgrain fan she tore out of the ceiling. A string of fairy lights and light from the kitchen is not quite enough light. With an Exacto blade, she trims back the wires' rubber skins by touch and guesswork. The coffee table squeaks and rattles with the weight of her, while a lightbulb rolls crazily at her feet.

Caution to the wind, Mary marvels. Lillian throws caution to the wind.

Lillian mates a light socket to the wires. Twists in the bulb. Fits the red globe over the dangling bulb. "Okay," she tells Mary. "Now."

Mary pushes the mother-of-pearl light switch. Red light rays out from the globe, streams down the walls.

"Ooh," says Mary.

"Ahh," says Lillian.

Brrraaat goes the doorbell.

They are thrilled to find Jenny sagging bonelessly in the doorway. "I've been in the public assistance line for seven hours," she says. "Seven. Hours." They coo at her reassuringly. She's on the dole after getting fired from the Artemis Cafe, then from Cafe Le Croissant, and again from the Lucky Penny coffeeshop. "Eek," she says, shrinking in the red light. "It's like hell in here."

"No, no," Mary insists. "Like wine. A waterfall of wine."

"Or blood," says Jenny, who has a bloodstain blooming on the seat of her pants.

Mary puts a throw pillow over the spot on the sofa where their cats regularly pee and pats the pillow to make Jenny come sit.

From the kitchen, Lillian shouts louder than she has to, "Mary, don't you dare tell about the beach."

Mary feels something in her eye. She takes off her glasses, tugs at her eyelid.

"Eek!" cries Jenny. "You turned your eyelid inside-out!"

Lillian plunks two tumblers of wine on the coffee table. Mary is bursting to tell the story of what they found at the beach, but Lillian cuts her off. "You wait, missy. I'm not finished in the kitchen."

Jenny furrows her brows and looks intensely at Mary. Jenny tells her, "Hold still," and leans close, sneaking her finger under the lens of Mary's glasses. Mary is startled by this intimacy. "Make a wish," says Jenny, offering Mary the eyelash upon her fingertip.

"You make a wish," says Mary. "You found it."

Jenny closes her eyes and blows. She takes Mary's foot onto her lap and pulls her toes one by one until each makes a little pop. Jenny purrs, "That's the first time I've seen you without your glasses. Take off your glasses again."

Blinking at the blur of Jenny, Mary says, "We made pumpkin pie yesterday."

"I was just about to offer her pie," Lillian crabs in the kitchen.

Jenny says, "Yes, pie. I'd love some pie." Then, "Good lord, I've bled down to my knees!"

"You certainly did," says Mary, putting her glasses back on.

"You knew? Why didn't you say something?"

"I assumed you didn't care. You're so devil-may-care."

"I *do* care." Jenny waddles off to the bathroom.

Mary calls after her, "I'm sure no one in the public assistance line cared. At least there's that."

From the bathroom, there comes another "Eek!"

Mary says, delighted, "Did you find a slug?"

"Yes."

When Jenny opens the bathroom door, Mary goes in, armed with a spatula, which she uses to pry the slug off the wall. She parades with it to the living room window and flips it out into the yard.

Lillian comes in with pie on a green glass dish in one hand, the other hand hidden behind her back. Jenny cannot hide her disappointment at the stinginess of her slice.

"Okay," says Lillian. "Now."

So Mary begins the story, but at *something dead* Jenny interrupts, "I don't want to hear this." Lillian launches into a description of the body and Jenny says, "Really, stop. Be nice. You're giving me the creeps."

They ask Jenny if she thinks it was vivisection, or Santeria!

Then Lillian draws the terrible hand out from behind her back, brandishes it at Jenny.

"The monkey's paw," says Mary. "You know the story. Make a wish!"

Curled up like a pill bug, Jenny says faintly, "Those wishes backfired."

Lillian says, very cheery, "Only because they were bad wishes."

"Make a wish, make a wish!" Mary chants, clapping her hands, full of the devil.

Jenny comes uncurled and seals her hand over Mary's mouth. "You found it, Mary—you make a wish."

Jenny leaves without drinking her wine. Through a mouthful of Jenny's unfinished pie, Mary says, "We are a monster," though secretly she thinks Jenny could use a thicker skin.

The day after, when Mary comes home from work, she and Lillian sit down on their ends of the sofa. Mary sniffs, "Our house is a catbox." She tells Lillian what she had for lunch, Vietnamese.

Lillian tells her she got rid of the hand. "I buried it."

"Funny, I heard the homophone of that, like you festooned it with berries." Mary waits for Lillian to smile. "So where did you bury it?"

"A good place." She won't tell where.

The hand wasn't hers to get rid of, Mary thinks. Bitterly, she does the dishes and makes a lot of noise doing them. Her distaste tastes awful, metallic.

Lillian slashes her mouth with lipstick and goes out, trailing perfume and Aquanet.

Mary rattles around the big apartment. There are four slugs and a mushroom in the bathroom. Fresh cat pee on the sofa. Someone is watching her through the living room window. What she sees is her own distorted reflection each time she checks the window to see if the bad man is gone.

Lillian doesn't come home.

When Mary gets back from the bookshop the next day, Lillian is sitting on her side of the sofa, hugging her knees, head tipped back, eyes closed. Her throat is jeweled with hickeys, cranberry-colored like her hair. Mary sweeps the living room, shoos the dust bunnies out from under the sofa, whacking the broom against the sofa legs.

Finally, Lillian says, "Some of us can't help it if we bruise like a peach."

Winding along the highway up the coast, the scenery is two-dimensional, unreal—rolling hills, dotted with cows, propped against the sky.

They park and hike down to the beach. Lillian has the blanket. Mary has wine in a paper bag. Across the water, under an afternoon moon, their city is a souvenir of itself.

In an alcove protected from the wind, where the shale has crumbled from the red cliff, they flop onto their stomachs, breathlessly, without bothering to spread the blanket. And the sand, just there, no place else, is littered with the airy corpses of monarch butterflies, dozens of them.

The best ones, the ones with wings intact, they choose and put carefully inside the paper bag. Mary wishes they had two bags.

The wings feel like ashes. Mary wishes Lillian would stay.

Lillian takes the butterflies and one of the cats. Mary asks Jenny to ask Lillian for some butterflies back.

A flattened and greasy white paper bag comes through Mary's mail slot. On it Lillian has written a note:

> *Here are flutterbys.*
> *Oh please can I have my half of the rental*
> *deposit. Me.*

Wanting Out

THE LADY on the phone wanted to know was I claustrophobic?

Fear of closets, I thought, Claustro the closet monster. I'm not afraid of my closet, though I am afraid of what's in it: clothes that don't fit, mostly, and clothes that do, fat clothes.

I said no. She said there'd be signs for Oncology/MRI, but the only signs I see say *tow-away physician parking only.*

Yesterday, when I got the call to remind me about my appointment, she asked again—claustrophobic? I should've said yes. I might've gotten some Valium out of it, like I get when I go to the dentist. One time, I made such a stink my dentist sent me flowers the next day, and that was just for a teeth-cleaning.

At last, a sign: Oncology/MRI, and a triangle pointing towards the cinderblock bunker with all the pipes and chimneys coming out of it, like a gas chamber.

I think positive: like a tanning bed. I pop a Nicorette into my mouth, on top of the piece I'm already chewing.

Inside, a skinny receptionist with skinny eyebrows—she looks like one of those halogen floor lamps—asks me, Are you claustrophobic? I shake my head. But I'm thinking there must be a reason they keep asking. She pushes a clipboard at me and smiles big. Her teeth are way too white. Blue-white, glowing.

I sit under the muddy painting of a barn, so I don't have to see it and think how much better I could've painted that barn, if I painted barns, if I were able to paint anymore, and I fill out the forms. Pacemaker? No. Metal pins or plates? No. Claustrophobic? N-O. Behind the glass, Floor Lamp and a blonde with fat flushed cheeks are laughing. Is this appropriate behavior? I mean, people are here to find out whether or not they've got, you know, cancer. The blonde flips her hair back. I picture her round red face with no hair.

I'm here because I can't smell. My doctor thinks something's pressing up against my hypothalamus. I'd heard of the hypothalamus but had no idea what it was or where, so I looked it up: *a basal part of the diencephalon that lies beneath the thalamus on each side, forms the floor of the third ventricle, and includes autonomic regulatory centers.*

Well.

A ventricle's part of the heart, right? And I thought: Phen-Fen. The Phen-Fen did something to my heart, but then I thought: what's the heart got to do with smell? Turns out brains have ventricles, too. Autonomic means involuntary reflexes, like blinking, breathing, the heartbeat. Digestion and pooping. Is smelling an involuntary reflex? If we can't help doing something, we just do it and do it, does that make it involuntary?

Egg salad. I don't know for how long my sense of smell's been gone, but making egg salad was when I knew.

The blonde comes through the double doors and calls my name, even though it's only me in here. I spit my Nicorette into my Nicorette baggie and follow her back through the double doors, then through another set of double doors posted with a big warning sign: a red horseshoe magnet with black lightning bolts coming out of it. I tell myself what I've been telling myself all day, that it'll be just like a tanning bed. Not like a microwave oven, a tanning bed.

This morning, I got the ring off finally. I was much thinner when I got married. Now there's a ring of white skin, and my finger cinches in, wasp-waisted.

The blonde talks at me, slow but perky, as if I don't speak English or I'm five, injecting each syllable with cheer. Have I ever had surgery? Surgery on my head? Any metal pins, plates, staples? Claustrophobic?

I've done time in the joint, in jail, so if I were claustrophobic I think I'd know.

I assumed the blonde was all red from laughing, but up close the redness is rosacea. I expect her to hand me a johnny or a paper gown. She doesn't. Don't I need to change? I ask. She tells me I'm fine. What about my shoes? Whatever's comfortable for you, she says. I keep my shoes on. She shows me through one more set of double doors, and there is a tremendous thumping, the machine has a heartbeat. Huge, the heartbeat and the machine itself, which is screaming *nuclear*, like, Hi! I'm going to rearrange your molecules! Mutate your DNA! Give you superpowers or give you cancer if you don't have it already! The blonde passes me off to a little brunette in a lab coat who looks about twelve, she could be selling makeup at the mall. The brunette pulls a stepstool up to the machine. I step on it and climb onto the paper-covered platform. Its tongue, my bed.

The brunette gives me a set of earplugs. I lie back and scooch along the paper-covered tongue until my head fits into the padded cradle. Then she locks my head into a cage and shouts—I can hardly hear over the *thunk! thunk! thunk!*—that this cage is the camera. She puts a rubber bulb in my hand. Squeeze, she shouts, if something's wrong. The cage-camera is tooth-colored, not the color of skinny Floor Lamp's teeth, actual tooth color.

The tongue starts to move, and the brunette yells, Tuck in your elbows! I strike a dead pose, holding the rubber bulb over my heart. I slide inside, and it *is* like a tanning bed, only I've never been on a tanning bed. But this is exactly how I imagine it would be—fluorescent, futuristic, lonely, and in the future there's no air. I can't get enough air.

If I have cancer, I bet my daughter will come home. And when the cancer gets to be too much, she'll know what to do: crush up my stockpile of pills, stir them into yogurt, feed me. And when I fall asleep, she'll slip a baggie over my head and beg me, Don't go, don't go, until my autonomic reflexes have stopped for good.

And Dan. Dan will be sorry when I've got a brain tumor the size of a grapefruit.

He used to nuzzle my hair when I'd gone a few days without shampooing. He'd breathe in deep and say, Sugar cone.

Not being able to smell yourself, it's a kind of numbness, like when your cheek is shot full of Novocain: you can bite it but it's like biting into nothing. I smell myself—nothing. I forget sometimes and sniff at a shirt to see if it needs washing. Nothing.

Why wash? Who cares?

Above me, there's a little wedge of mirror, and in it I can see my—lord, this is *loud.* Like ray guns, a hundred ray guns going off at once, on top of the thunking. In the mirror I can see my feet. Hello feet. On the mirror are spatters of something like toothpaste. Fear sweat, maybe. Or tears.

My tongue keeps fiddling with my chipped front tooth. I grind my teeth in my sleep. If I was asleep and there was a fire, I wouldn't wake up from the smoke smell. I wouldn't smell the smoke smell. When you can't smell, cooking's hard. Like cookies, you know they're done when they smell done. If you can't smell and you're baking cookies and you forget you can't smell and you can't get up off the sofa, you can't get up to paint like you were going to, like you were going to every day for the past two years, and it's a beautiful day out but your drapes are closed, your eyes are closed, you're catatonic on the sofa waiting till the cookies smell done—forget it. You'll know they're done, or done for, when your eyes start to burn from the smoke. I almost burnt the house down yesterday afternoon, only it was brownies, not cookies. Double-fudge.

The Louderbachs across the street winter in Arizona. I water their plants while they're away. The Louderbachs are my only neighbors, unless you count the Adairs down the road, but they're RV people, so they're home even less than the Louderbachs. If I'm asleep and there's a fire, I'm done for.

I did get up off the sofa in October. I went on a road trip. I even painted some.

I used to paint flowers. Now, I don't paint anything, and my garden's gone to seed, and I can't even smell flowers anymore.

My daughter hates my paintings. Too many flowers, she says. I cram too many flowers into one painting. She says my flower paintings make her claustrophobic. I call it attention to detail.

I'm forgetting what flowers smelled like. I'm forgetting what it was like to smell. I tell myself it was my brain getting a taste of something. Everybody knows about smell and memory, how smells can take you back. But I forget why I threw the coffeepot at Dan's head two years ago. He ducked and it hit the wall, shattered. For my birthday, he got me a metal coffeepot

and laughed, and I said, Get out. He put some things in a duffel bag, took a case of beer from the pantry, and I watched from
the living room window as he started up his truck and peeled
out of the driveway. And pulled across the street into the Louderbachs' driveway.

What I'd had in mind: Danny-boy sweating it out at the
Super 8 and calling me all apologetic, then we'd talk dirty. But
it was winter and the Louderbachs were away, so that's where
he stayed.

Now I remember why I threw the coffeepot: an egg salad
sandwich. I'd taken out a hundred-thousand-dollar life insurance policy on Dan, and shortly after that I fixed him an egg
salad sandwhich. He sniffed at it, sure it was bad. He was convinced I was trying to kill him with egg salad. It smelled fine to
me.

Dan's truck always stank of sour, rotten beer. He drank and
drove, and threw the empties behind the seat. Time to time, I'd
clear out the cans, two trashbags full, and take them to the
recycling center where all the retarded people work.

Years ago, when I was hugely pregnant, I was at the beach
with my also pregnant friend Maureen, whose name back then
was Indrani (she got her spiritual name from a waiter at a
Malaysian restaurant). All along the shore were dead jellyfish
like silicone breasts, probably live ones in the water, but the
water was so warm. We were the only ones there, and it was
the 1960s, so we waded in naked. Then a schoolbus pulled up,
and a busload of retarded people flocked into the water. They
made a circle around us and put their hands on our bellies,
gently. It was like we'd landed on another planet.

We both had girls. Maureen did one of those underwater
births, only her baby was underwater too long. Her baby was
brain damaged. But I never met a happier baby, always smiling

and shaking with orgasms of pure happiness. Her daughter will never leave home. My daughter got as far away from me as she could get.

Taking space, she calls it. She took 3,000 miles of space.

When I phoned and said her dad had left, she said, Oh, thank God. She said, Good. She said, It's about time someone in this family started making some healthy choices.

I said, Healthy Choices, isn't that a brand of TV dinner?

From our living room, I watched Dan watching TV in the Louderbachs' living room. When I called the Louderbachs' number, Dan got up from Mr. Louderbach's chair and picked up the phone. He said, Hello? Hello?

I didn't say anything, just listened then hung up.

When I called the Louderbachs in Arizona and told them Dan was living in their house, they said, That's fine. As long as he waters the plants.

Dan watched a lot of TV, same as he did at home. He kept the drapes open. I kept the lights off so he couldn't see me watching. But he knew. He started smoking again, and he flaunted it. He smoked right out front in the Louderbachs' driveway. We'd quit together. I replaced cigarettes with Nicorette. But what replaces Dan?

Not art. I've been working, or not working, on the same painting for two years now. Before, I averaged three paintings a month. "Bearded Irises" was supposed to be my "Sunflowers." For a while, I went to a support group for blocked artists, but all we did was play Pictionary.

Food replaced Dan a long time ago. But food, like Dan, has lost its zing. Now that I can't smell, I can barely taste. Salad's like chewing on wet paper towels. And yesterday's brownies, had they survived, would've tasted like chocolate-ish sponges. Taste or no, I overdo it anyway.

One night, the Louderbachs' drapes were closed. Next to Dan's truck in the driveway was one of those cute new VW Bugs. Stuffed tiger in the back window. Dried roses on the dash. Nail in her tire.

Another night, Dan had a party. I called the Louderbachs in Arizona. They said, That's fine. As long as he doesn't burn the house down. I saw rivers of gasoline sloshed on the Louderbachs' driveway, Dan stumping out a cigarette. Of course, I didn't do *that*. I'm no firebug. Instead, I went over to the Louderbachs' with a six-pack. Dan was bent over his guitar. Hey, Dan-o, I said, Dan the Man. He kept on noodling with his guitar. None of our friends would speak to me, they wouldn't even look at me. I was invisible. I sat next to the girl in the sequin-eyed cat sweatshirt—Little Miss Female, I presumed— and introduced myself as The Wife. To be nice, I handed her a beer. I said, Do I know you?

She said, I clean your teeth.

I squeezed her arm, nicely, and said, I just thought of the perfect bumper sticker for you.

She blew into her bottle, making a mournful *hoot*.

I laughed, Dental hygienists do it orally!

Dan said, Go. Go, or I'm calling the cops.

It's—quiet. Quieter, anyway. There's still the pounding sound, but the ray guns have quit firing, and the tongue is on the move. I'm out, I'm out, I'm out. A man with glasses greets me, Don't move! Hearing the voice, I realize he's a mannish woman, and German. Don't move, she commands. I wonder what happened to the little brunette. This one takes away the rubber bulb and pushes my sleeve up to my armpit. Snaps a tourniquet around my arm and tells me to make a fist. She's waving a foot-long needle. She says, Die. *What?* High-contrast dye, she says louder, to help us see you better. She takes forever cotton-balling the inside of my elbow before the needle bites in.

I get my rubber bulb back. I forget already how loud it's going to be. Smoke alarm loud, like I am wearing smoke alarm earmuffs.

So, the weather got warmer and the Louderbachs came home, like ducks. Dan went someplace else. Now, I thought, now I will break the habit of Dan. I primered over "Bearded Irises" and started again from scratch. My doctor put me on the Phen-Fen (yes, I know, heart damage, but I didn't know that then). I jazzercised. I got into therapy. *My paid friend,* I called my therapist. For a while, I was up.

Then one day Dan stopped by. For sex. But Mr. Closed Mouth wouldn't say where he was living, even after the sex. After that, I couldn't get off the sofa for weeks.

I called my daughter. She said, I can't believe you slept together. What were you thinking?

He complimented my paintings, I said. Don't I deserve to be happy?

She said, What does your shrink think about this?

I told her, My paid friend thinks you need to call me more often. She says you need to call me every day. What if I died? Who would know I was dead? If I die, it's gonna be ugly. I mean, it's gonna be weeks and weeks before somebody finds me. Weeks.

My daughter said, The mailman will figure it out.

I skipped therapy, again, and drove over to Dan's work, waited for him to get done for the day. I followed his truck home. Home was a pink stucco box, like a brick of strawberry ice cream, with a rock garden out front. That Bug was in the driveway.

Halloween was coming. When our daughter was thirteen, Dan and I sacrificed two good sheets and secretly went as ghosts to her junior high Halloween dance. She was dressed as a magenta-haired punk, with black lips and fingernails, Goodwill clothes, and piles of junk jewelry (soon enough, she'd be dressing that way every day). Dan disguised his voice and asked her to dance, but she said no. When she got home, we were waiting on the sofa, wearing our sheets. The look on her face.

On Halloween, I showed up on Little Miss Female's doorstep, draped in a sheet. A black cat was thumbtacked to the door. I pushed the buzzer. Dan opened the door, flashing plastic fangs at me, red goo smeared down the corners of his mouth. I held out a pillowcase and said, Trick or treat! He dropped a bite-size Snickers into the pillowcase and shut the door in my face. When I got home, I just sat in my flowers, furiously weeding in the dark, and that's when the smell hit me, my brain got a taste of something awful. I flipped on the porch light. Under my Sterling Silver rosebush, cat poo.

Late the next morning, I headed over to Little Miss Female's. The driveway was empty, so I set to work hunting for the spare key. Under the doormat was too obvious, but I lifted it anyway. I felt along the top of the doorframe, checked the mailbox, upturned several suspicious rocks. No hidden key. Next door, someone was cleaning the blinds with a very small squeegee. So what if someone was watching me. I tried the doorknob. Open.

Inside, how perfect: cats. Hundreds, no, thousands of cats. Not actual cats, figurines. Six-deep on the mantel, littlest kitties in front, tall swan-necked ones at the back, a theater of cats— how did she dust them all? Elsewhere, cat-head ashtrays, leopard-print throw pillows, and on the TV, a Siamese cat lamp with blue rhinestone eyes.

Dan can't stand cats. He hates them more than broccoli, even more than garlic, which he always said tasted like feet. Now I can cook with all the garlic I want, but fat lot of good this does since I can't taste it exactly. It's a symbolic gesture.

Upon opening Little Miss Female's medicine cabinet, hoping to find evidence of fungus or psychosis, I came face-to-face with a diaphragm case and a huge tube of spermicidal jelly, squashed flat. I took the double-baggied cat poo out of my purse and emptied it onto the floor behind the toilet, where no one would ever think to look.

Time to time, Dan would stop by. For some of his things. For sex. I got off the sofa that winter only to water the Louderbachs' plants, and when they came home in the spring, I didn't get off the sofa at all.

I received the annual Xeroxed newsletter from Maureen, who was running a colon-cleansing retreat in upstate New York: wheat grass and enemas and wheat grass enemas. Camp Doody, she called it. At the bottom was a handwritten note inviting me to come detoxify. She still dotted her i's with bubbles. She also wrote, My kid got her black belt in Aikido. She is like Alice in Wonderland, the innocence of the universe. Sweet and lovey as ever. How's yours?

I said to myself, I have no idea.

My daughter was a schoolteacher in Vermont, a day's drive from Camp Doody. Back when I was still seeing my paid friend, she'd said I needed a project, a purpose. She'd said that till she was blue in the face.

So, I got myself up off the sofa and prepared to hit the open road. In my minivan, my ark, I built a plywood platform with a piece of foam to sleep on, and plenty of storage underneath for art supplies and snacks. I emptied the contents of my medicine cabinet into baggies. By now, everybody knew about

Phen-Fen and heart attacks. My doctor continued to prescribe it on the sly.

Wyoming had the best pie, and Yellowstone, that was *really* like being on another planet. The geyser part. Then there's the woodsy part, where I hiked with a group of German tourists who all started whistling when we came upon a pile of fresh bear poo. Apparently you're supposed to whistle if you run into a bear. I can't whistle, so I got my pepper spray out of my fanny-pack and sang *dooby dooby doo*.

Mount Rushmore, I decided, is 10,000-years-from-now's Sphinx.

My mistake was taking the shortcut through Canada. I'd wanted to make it to Camp Doody by nightfall. I tried to cross the border just outside of Detroit. The sky was green. When the Mountie asked me to pull over, I joked that I was his big drug bust. I was kidding. When the Mountie put me in handcuffs, I screamed something about calling *60 Minutes* and Diane Sawyer. When I got my one phone call, I didn't call *60 Minutes*, I called my cousin the lawyer.

They'd found my dolls—Codeine, Percocet, Vicodin, Valium, Xanax, and, yes, Phen-Fen—and they arrested me for having prescription drugs without the prescriptions. I told them I *did* have prescriptions, just not on me, and the drugs were in baggies to take up less space.

Meanwhile, I was manacled to a six-foot-tall woman named Cookie and hauled off to a holding cell, which smelled like throw-up and was littered with undrunk boxes of orange drink and plastic-wrapped hamburgers, rock-hard from the microwave. I lined the hamburgers and boxes of orange drink neatly along the perimeter of the cell. There was a sink and a toilet, but no toilet paper, and my bed was a slab of concrete.

For dinner, Cookie and I got microwaved hamburgers and

boxes of orange drink, but no poky straws with which to open our juice boxes because we might use the straws as weapons. They also took away my shoelaces, as if I might try to hang myself with shoelaces. That night, I had no pillow or blanket, so I yelled, Guard, guard! and Cookie said, You have to say constable, so I yelled, Constable, constable! and when I asked for a pillow and a blanket, and could he please get me some Nicorette out of my purse, the constable said, What do you think this is, the Ritz? I slept with my head on my shoes. Same shoes I have on now, the ones I can see in the little mirror above me.

Breakfast was more hamburgers and orange drink. My cousin the lawyer found me a lawyer in Canada, whose name was Dick Champion, a name I thought boded well. I met Dick Champion in the morning before my bail hearing. There was a slight problem. The Phen-Fen had tested positive for morphine, and they weren't likely to be lenient about morphine. The charges: possession of narcotics with intent to distribute— me, a drug trafficker!—and possession of a concealed weapon, my pepper spray. Bail was set at $10,000, and Dick Champion got busy hitting up my relatives. Thing is, I really did smuggle drugs once, years ago, young and stupid and reeking of patchouli, coming back from India with Indrani. These sticky wads of opium, *bong balls* they called them in India, we'd put some bong balls in baggies and tucked them up inside us for the flight home. I, of course, got my period.

Cookie had a scar on her temple, shaped like a peach pit, like she'd been slammed upside the head with a peach pit. I didn't ask how she got it. She'd gone after her husband with a knife and stabbed him, but it couldn't have been a very deep cut because her bail was only $500, which was still more than she could afford, and her husband certainly wasn't going to put up the money.

Cookie and I were chained together again, then put in a van and taken to Canadian jail. Compared to the holding cell, jail *was* the Ritz. There were cots with mattresses and pillows, and there was a bathroom with a door you could close. And the food—we got peanut butter! Fruit cocktail! Chili for dinner and cherry cobbler for dessert!

I told my chain-smoking cellmates, Whatever you do, no matter how much I beg, *do not* give me a cigarette. Angela, a cute little thing with braids and a farmgirl face, held up a liquor store with a ski mask on and a knife in one hand, a gun in the other. She was hoping to get out and go to London for her daughter's birthday. I said, Wow, you have a daughter living in London? And she said, London, *Ontario*. Then there was Shirl, our leader, the powerful one. When I asked Shirl what she was in for, she said, None of your damn business. Eventually, she warmed up to me, sort of, even lent me one of her books to read, though she got to pick which one. *Eye of the* something, *Cry of the* something, I forget.

After a week of wearing the same underpants, the week I was supposed to be cleansing my colon at Camp Doody, I made bail. I hugged my cellmates good-bye. Cookie and I cried, and I promised I'd get her out.

The hills of Vermont were on fire with fall colors, and I would've stopped to paint them except I was in a hurry to make it to my daughter's school by Halloween.

For Halloween this year, I dressed as a headless person. I had on a raincoat of Dan's, stuffed with clothes to pad the shoulders, lifting them up over my head. On my head, covering my face, I wore a black t-shirt, filling in the vee between the lapels, blacking out the space where a head would normally be. I could see through the black fabric, but barely.

A student aide in the office led me to my daughter's

classroom. I sat in the back and unzipped my knapsack, pretending to rummage for a pen and paper.

Enigma, my daughter said. The student who came in tardy is an enigma. Enigma.

Teacher, someone shouted, who *is* that?

She made the settle-down gesture, patting the air down.

I held my camera up to my eyes, but I couldn't find the viewfinder through the black fabric.

In a low, flat voice she said, Mother.

Surprise!

I got out of my costume and snapped her picture. I handed out candy, I was the Halloween Fairy, and her students absolutely loved me. My daughter said, I'm in the middle of giving a vocabulary quiz. Then, quieter, You shouldn't have come.

My paid friend said I should come, I lied.

My daughter said, You have to go.

I told her, You have to be nice to me. I just spent a week in jail. My cellmates all said I should come.

She shushed me, flapping her hands, slapping the air down.

I just wanted to see you teach. If I asked, you would've said no.

Please, she said. Go.

The noise stops, though not the infernal thumping, that never stops, and I am spit out very slowly. I ache from stillness. Holding one position for so long *hurts*. The German woman with glasses lifts the cage off my head.

On my way out, I ask the receptionist, the Floor Lamp, if they'll call me if anything bad shows up on my MRI. She shrugs and says, I assume so.

I had to fly back to Canada for my trial. In the end, all the drug charges were dropped, though I did have to pay a $200 fine for the pepper spray. I never did bail Cookie out.

The sky is purple. I'm really working my gum to get the juice. Overhead, there's an enormous black cloud, but nobody said anything about rain. Birds. A cloud of birds, wheeling like bits of burnt paper. Crows, millions. What do they call it, a murder of crows? This is a holocaust. Every inch of every branch, every power line has a bird on it. Do crows migrate? Do they? The black cloud keeps coming.

One of Us

WE HAVE separate beds, but sometimes we sleep in one bed, stomach to stomach, the way we were born. Hussein jerks and kicks, dreaming. I kick him back.

"Has*san*," he groans into his flower pillow, giving it a punch between our heads that sends up a puff of sunlit dust.

Pulling apart our sweaty stomachs almost hurts, like pulling off a bandage. "Hey, Sleeping Beauty," I say, rolling on top of him, out of bed. "Hey, fathead. Open your eyes. Wake up, wake up."

Hussein says, "Shut up, shut up," and pulls the blankets over his face.

I hop over to get my crutches. Mine are shinier than his, less dinged-up. I rip the blankets off of him and sing, "Good morning to you, you smell like a zoo!" and then I get out of there fast before he finds something to throw at me.

The kitchen table is covered with bread slices. Every morning, Monday to Friday, our mother makes the Sandwich of the Day for our family's store. She wears her pink bathrobe and plastic gloves, her hair stuffed into a blue paper shower cap, the kind they wear in hospitals. Before we came here for the operation, before she became American, she kept her hair hid under a head scarf. Cranking open a gallon can of tuna, she tilts her head at a jar of pickle relish, meaning open it. I try. "Mama, I can't."

"Go ask your brother," she says, so I try harder. The lid feels greased. My palm is dented, all red and white. I hold it up to show her. Spooning tuna into a giant metal bowl, she says again, "Go ask your brother."

I have a trick up my sleeve. I whack the lid with the can opener, then, *pop!* the lid twists off easy, and I hold up the jar, victorious. My mother isn't paying attention, she's mixing mayonnaise into the tuna with her hands. I get some yogurt and take it into the family room. On the container Clo the Cow, the Clover Dairy mascot, bites a four-leaf clover like a Spanish dancer bites a rose.

Soon Mrs. Marchant will be here to drive us to school. Mrs. Martian, the teacher's aide. We go to a one-room schoolhouse out in the country—white with a white picket fence, a bell, and a blue door—the postcard-picture of a country schoolhouse. Oscar Mayer made a commercial at our school, and we got to be extras and eat about a hundred hot dogs apiece; at our house, we don't eat pork.

We're the only kids in our grade, sixth, the top grade, which makes us the bosses of our school. In the fall, when we go to junior high, there will be four hundred kids in our grade.

Where we were born in Africa, all boy twins are named Hassan and Hussein. Here, it's just us, sore thumbs with our one legs and strange names. When we were littler and still played with dolls, we always pulled off one of the legs so the dolls would look like us. *Action figures,* Hussein would say, or *guys,* not dolls.

I slide my arm out of the cuff of my crutch. In the fog my breath makes on the window next to the front door, I write my name. A ladder of English letters, then Arabic: Hassan, the name always given to the twin born first. We were born at exactly the same time. Our mother will be annoyed by the fingerprints on the glass, and she'll know who, it's my name, so I mop the window with my shirt. I breathe on it again and write my brother's name. Our names are the only words I know how to write in Arabic. I bang my lunchbox against my leg.

At last, Mrs. Martian pulls up and honks *doo doo doo,* which our mother hates; she says, why should the whole street know it's time for Hassan and Hussein to go to school?

I get shotgun, I'm there first. Shotgun, that's what Hussein calls the front seat. Him and his soccer friends fight over who gets the front seat—whoever yells shotgun first sits up front. Hussein's the athlete, the outdoorsy type. I like to read. All buckled-up in the front seat, shotgun, waiting for my brother, like always, it's impossible not to imagine what if. What if we hadn't been separated. Maybe it would hurry him up. Maybe I'd spend my whole life waiting.

Sometimes I dream that Chang and Eng come and stick us together again. *We weren't separated,* says Chang. *So why should you be?* says Eng. Chang and Eng are the bosses of all Siamese twins. Actually, they were born in China.

Mrs. Martian honks again and unwedges her coffee from between her seat and the emergency brake. Every morning, she gets a coffee from Z's Fairwest Market. Our father is Z. At Christmastime, he gives a bottle of wine to each of his best customers, and Mrs. Martian gets wine every year, I bet, because of all the lottery tickets and crushed to-go cups padding the car floor under my foot.

"So," says Mrs. Martian. "As of yesterday, I'm a grandma."

I'm not sure whether this is good news or bad news.

Here's Hussein, the slowpoke, pole vaulting on his crutches, swinging himself in big Olympic leaps across our red lawn of lava rocks. Mrs. Martian starts up the car, then our mother comes running outside in her robe, waving a yogurt and a spoon. Hussein's breakfast. "Be good," says our mother. *Be good*, like mothers about to die in fairy stories always say to their kids. She gives Hussein a forehead kiss good-bye.

We pull away from the curb, and Mrs. Martian says, "They named him Jupiter. *Jupiter*, what kind of name is that?"

I tell Hussein, "Mrs. Marchant became a grandmother yesterday."

Mrs. Martian hunches over the steering wheel, squinting down her nose through glasses that are like thick circles drawn on with Magic Marker. "I said to my son, what are you going to call him for short? *Jew?*"

My seatbelt suddenly strangles me. Hussein is stepping on my seatbelt. I slap his foot away, and he moves it onto the hump between the front seats. His shoe is dirty white. Mine is silver. Our mother says our feet are growing so fast we look like the letter L. "Jupiter," I say, "is the Roman name for Zeus, god of thunder and lightning, the king of the gods."

"That's right," says Mrs. Martian, taking the last sip of coffee then dropping the empty cup on the car floor, my side. I stomp it flat.

Hussein says, "Egghead," meaning me.

"Fathead," I shoot back.

"Boys," warns Mrs. Martian.

Hussein ignores her. "Know-it-all," he calls me, digging his chin into my shoulder, his breath hot in my ear. I know more about Zeus than I do about Mohammed, and we were named after his twin grandsons. I know more about Mrs. Martian's grandson's name than I do about my own.

After the flashing yellow light at Sunnyside Road, the houses stop, and the golden hills and smell of cows begin. When we come to the farm where all the cows are black with white middles, like Oreo cookies, Mrs. Martian says, "Do those cows have halos? Because I'm seeing halos."

"Zeus turned one of his girlfriends into a cow," I say, "to hide her from his wife. In another story, he turned *himself* into a cow. And with another girl, he became a swan. She laid eggs and hatched twins."

Hussein huffs at me and pops the lid off his yogurt.

"Well, I'm seeing halos," says Mrs. Martian. "That's it, I'm going blind."

Hussein leans forward, and with his mouth full he says, "No, Mrs. M, you're not going blind. Your windshield's just filthy."

I wipe my finger on the glass, leaving a clean clear streak. My fingertip is brown.

He says, "I'm seeing halos too."

"Yeah, me too," I say, rubbing the grime off my finger onto my blue shorts, the empty leg; where I touched the windshield, the sky is almost as blue. We've got prosthetic legs, but they don't fit, we're growing so fast. They're not like shoes, we can't go out and get new legs whenever we outgrow them. The car xylophones over the metal bars of a cattle grate.

When we put on prosthetic legs, dressing them up in shoes and socks like doll legs, we walk like Frankensteins—we get around better without them—but people don't stare as much and laugh and point or whatever. I'd stare at us too. Actually, the main reason for wearing them is to keep people from always, always, asking why we each have one leg. People are curious is all. Still, I'd like a new leg for junior high.

A leaf darts out into the road, and Mrs. Martian brakes and swerves. She says, "Did I hit it? Did I hit it?"

"It was just a leaf," I say. Hussein gives me his yogurt to hold and pulls himself up off the floor of the backseat, mouthing *ow, ow,* massaging his bony backside, and I tell him to put on his seatbelt. I'm trying not to laugh.

My backside isn't sore because his is. It's not like if you prick Hussein with a pin then I will feel it. We don't have ESP or any other mumbo jumbo; one of us isn't the good one, one of us isn't bad.

We don't remember being Siamese, before we were separated. We were babies.

"See," says Mrs. Martian. "I *am* going blind. And my doctor says I've got to go in for another colonoscopy for my irritable bowel." She chuckles, "I call it my *irascible* bowel." I smile and nod like I get her joke.

We come to the last and biggest hill before school. Up, up, and over the top, my stomach drops as we slide down the side of the great big bowl of land all spread out beneath us: amber waves of grass not waving, and cows, and far off on clear days like today is, purple mountain majesties. Barreling along faster, faster, I feel so free, so light, like we might lift off and fly into the for spacious sky, and then one of us says, "Holy cow."

A reddish-brown and white cow, spang in the middle of the road. We scream, the brakes scream, there's a sickening chemical smell. We are headed smack for the wall of cow, and I curl up and duck, slamming my foot against an imaginary brake, eyes shut, waiting for the crash.

My rubberband neck cracks forward, snaps back—and we're stopped. A ghost of the cow is branded inside my eyelids. My hand is wet and I'm scared to open my eyes and see all the blood. I open one eye a little. I see the cow scrambling up out of a ditch; we didn't hit it. Then the other eye. Spiderweb crack on the windshield; the crack sound wasn't my neck, it was my brother's head hitting the glass. He is slumped face-down between the front seats. The blood on my hand is yogurt.

We are going to be late for school.

My brother is not moving.

I give him a shake. He does not move. To break the spell, I cover him with kisses. "Wake up," I chant between kisses. "Wake up. Wake up. Come on, open your eyes."

"Cut it off," he says, coming to life, swatting at me. "Knock it out."

"You were knocked out," I tell him. "You scared the life out of me—I thought you were dead. From now on wear your seatbelt, okay?"

"Duh." He sits up slowly, wiping his neck where I kissed. Quick, I kiss his ear; punishment for *duh,* for making me so afraid.

Mrs. Martian says, weirdly cheer-uppy, "That's some goose egg you got there, Hussein." Then her face collapses into lines. She starts bumping her head on the steering wheel, knocking her glasses farther and farther down her nose. "They ought to put me out to pasture."

"It's not your fault there was a cow in the road," I say. "It's not your fault Hussein wasn't wearing his seatbelt, it's his." I turn to Hussein and give him a look, like *say something,* but he just sits there scowling in the backseat. His forehead is huge, like a baby doll, and I can't keep looking or I'll laugh. I scratch Mrs. Martian behind the ear, like she's a dog, because it's the only thing I can think of to do.

"Let's go to school," I say. I can see the bell tower from here. We are *so* late.

"No," she says, and if she were a dog her ears would've pricked up. "I've got to get Hussein to the hospital."

"But I'm fine," he whines.

"No," says Mrs. Martian. "You could have a concussion. Or a fractured skull. Or your brain could be bleeding, mister." She taps her forehead at him in the rearview mirror. "Put on your seatbelt. Now."

Hussein says, "You'd think if your brain was bleeding it would let you know."

I say, "May I please go to school?" I think I see the school bell swinging. I think I hear it ringing.

A Clover Milk truck, a semi with silver tanks, blasts its horn and thunders by, rocking us like a toy boat. On the side was Clo the Cow prancing on her hind legs in a flowerbed. *Tip Clo through your two lips,* it said underneath. Every time I blink, I see the cow we almost hit; the colors of dried blood and bandages. I bust up laughing. Tip Clo! Two lips! My brother's giant forehead! His fat, fat head. I laugh so hard I feel sick to my stomach.

When they drop me off at school, the last thing Hussein says before they speed away is: "If we get to the hospital thirty seconds too late and I die it's your fault, egghead."

Chang died of a blood clot in his brain, probably. Eng died an hour after, maybe of fright, or else because all the blood flowed out of him into the dead body of Chang. Their wives didn't want doctors sawing up the brothers' bodies, so no one knows for sure.

UNION SCHOOL EST. 1874. That we modern-day separate Siamese twins go to a school called Union is freaky, but what's even freakier, it was built the exact same year that Chang and Eng died. I climb the hundred-year-old wooden steps. Pull the blue door open. Inside, they are finishing the Pledge, and little Luis Ortiz looks over at me, sucking several fingers that should be on his heart, while everyone else faces the flag as they recite, "One nation under God, indivisible, with liberty and justice for all." Then they all turn from the flag to face me.

"We had an accident," and as I'm saying this, I feel like the captain of the ship, it's my job to keep everyone calm, everything under control. "Hussein's on the way to the hospital. Nothing to worry about, just a bump on the head." I tell the little ones, miming for those who don't know English, "Always wear your seatbelts."

I ask our teacher, Mrs. O, may I phone my mother, and I call her—she's anything but calm. When I say not to worry, it's just a bump on the head, she hangs up on me. I'm guessing she flew out of the house to catch a bus to the hospital, still wearing her pink robe (I see it flapping open, showing her naked legs, and her not caring) and blue paper shower cap (I hear the crinkle and scrape of paper loud in her ears, I hear that and her breathing, her heart beating fast, as she runs for the bus).

I hang up the phone, and Mrs. O cries, "Oh, oh," smothering me in a hug. She smells like flowers, lots and lots of flowers. She lets me go then announces that we will have a moment of silence to pray for Hussein.

"Really," I say, "he's okay."

And Mrs. O says, "Good thoughts never hurt."

So everyone sits at their desks, eyes closed. When I close my eyes there are gory splotches of reddish-brown and white. Mrs. O's perfume is caught in my nose, in my throat, too many flowers choking me. I pray this moment of silence will hurry up and end.

My Sandwich of the Day, tuna fish, tastes like salty soggy newspapers, and it's warm from sitting in my cubby all morning long. Nobody's called from the hospital. My brother could be dead, or in a coma, for all I know. He's not dead, he's not in a coma, but somebody should at least call and let me know.

Earlier, Mrs. O had me help the littlest kids with Math, like Mrs. Martian does usually. It was easy stuff, just plus and take away, how many apples and oranges, but Luis Ortiz and his brother Guillermo, who's called Bill, don't speak English yet. I had to show them with blocks. Lucky for me, my parents already spoke some English when we came here.

After I got the little ones started in their workbooks, I tried to do my own Math, word problems, distance equals rate times time, but I couldn't concentrate: if we're hurtling downhill at fifty miles an hour, fifteen miles over the speed limit, and the cow's a hundred feet away, how hard does Hussein's head hit the windshield?

If Mrs. Martian drives eleven miles to Valley Hospital, doing thirty-five the whole way, how long does it take them to get there? If my brother dies, whose fault is it?

I chuck my sandwich into the trashcan. That's a Hussein word, *chuck;* I throw, he chucks. Front seat, shotgun.

Somehow, my brother always keeps me waiting.

A seagull, far from any sea, dive-bombs my sandwich. Missy Harelik (as in Harelik Farms Milk) and April-Dawn Purdy are having a contest on the bars, who can do the most cherry twirls in a row. They dip upside-down and flip back up, pinwheeling round and round, while everyone counts. Missy's hair whips the dirt, April-Dawn's does not; her head was shaved last year when she had lice. They have the same contest every lunchtime. I tear myself away from this excitement.

"Valley Hospital," a lady answers. "How may I direct your call?"

"I'm calling about a patient."

She says, "We can't give out patient information over the phone."

"But he's my brother." *My Siamese twin brother, you idiot lady.* She's sorry, she says. "Mrs. Lady," I say, "Please?"

I hear a heavy breath and tapping, a pen maybe, or fingernails. "Let me see if I can get the doctor for you. What's the patient's last name?" I say it and spell it out, then I'm on hold, listening to some plink-plink music, waiting.

Nobody knows why twins twin, what makes the egg split in two. Let alone why the egg divides and does not quite make two, like Chang and Eng, or why in our case the egg gave up at one and a half.

Mrs. O is ringing the bell to tell everyone lunch is over. I almost don't notice someone on the phone yelling faintly, "Hello? Hello?"

"I'm here, I'm here," I say. "I can't hear you."

Between clangs of the bell, I make out the word *discharged*, as everyone charges through the blue door, stampeding to their desks. And who follows, herding them inside like a sheepdog, but Mrs. Martian, collared by a foam neck brace. To the phone I say, "Okay yes thank you, gotta go." There is no Hussein following after her.

Mrs. O, done ringing, makes the simmer-down gesture, patting the air down with her hands. On the blackboard she draws a road that starts wide and ends in a point. Instead of getting news about my brother, we get a lecture about perspective in Art. I sit on my hands, bite my tongue.

Meanwhile, Mrs. Martian unrolls butcher paper and cuts a sheet for each of us, then she pours tempera paints into egg cartons. She comes around to every desk, laying down a place setting of paint and paper, and when she finally comes to mine, she says, "Your brother's home now with your mama. He has a slight concussion."

When she comes to my desk again on her next go-round giving out brushes, I ask, "What's a concussion?"

"He bumped his brain a little." She knights me on the head with a paintbrush.

I dip my brush in black. I paint two stick figures, side by side, one leg each. I paint green hills around us. I've done nothing to show perspective, so I paint a large fence in the foreground. At the top of the page I write TWINS. The paint is too wet, we bleed together. The fence looks like a cage.

At home Hussein's watching *The Price Is Right,* whirling his flower pillow like a propeller over his head. His flower pillow, which is maroon flannel, not flowered anymore, is his security blanket.

"Seven-oh-one!" he shouts at the TV. He's surprisingly good at this game show.

His head has shrunk down since this morning but something about him is not right. Still swollen between his eyebrows. He doesn't look like himself.

Our mother is in the doorway, eyes looking puffy and boiled. A wood doll with a head like a dish is tucked under the sash of her robe, held to her stomach. "Hussein?" she says. "You say something?"

I tell her, "He's playing a game show, Mama." If he was playing for real, he'd have just won golf clubs.

"Hussein?" she says. "You need anything?"

He tosses his flower pillow in the air and catches it. "I could go for a fruit pie," he says.

To me she says, "Be a good brother. Go fetch your brother a fruit pie."

"Lemon," he says.

Here I go again: what if. I wouldn't be headed down the block to Z's Fairwest Market, fetching my brother a fruit pie, if not for the separation. And we wouldn't be separated if not for the Anonymous Donor. This must be how adopted kids feel, having parents with blurry faces they can only imagine. If not for the Anonymous Donor, there might not even be a *we,* and we certainly wouldn't be living here; we'd be where there are flesh-eating diseases, famines, and machete massacres, where they chop off the hands of thieves and stone disobedient women to death.

The dish-headed doll is an ancient custom. There are two of them, twins, one for each of us. When one twin is sick, the mother binds his doll to her stomach, keeping him there until he's healed.

When we were born, I was the strong one. So the story goes. Our mother wore Hussein's doll as he weakened and grew small. We shared veins, blood; no matter how much I fattened up, if he died, so would I. Separation was the only choice; cut off the dying brother so the other could live. What kind of choice is that?

All together it took thirteen doctors to take us apart. After the operation a funny thing happened: soon as he was free from me, Hussein became the strong one. I went on a breathing machine.

On the corner where Fair Street meets Western Avenue is Z's Fairwest Market. Inside, my father looks up from his ledger to greet me, "Hassan, my man."

"Hey, Baba." I scan the rack of fruit pies for lemon. Normally, Hussein prefers cherry.

The bells tied to the front door clatter and clink, and my father says, "Smiley, my man," greeting the old toothless guy who comes by to refill the gumball machines with candy and toy trinkets.

"What's shaking, Z?" Then Smiley thrusts his hand at me. "Give me five, buddy. Slip me some skin." I let go of a crutch and slap his leathery palm.

Unlocking the gumball machines, he gives me a wink, tells me to pick out any toy I want. I choose a yellow devil head charm.

Smiley's van rumbles off in a cloud of blue smoke. My father picks up a stack of envelopes and says, "Mind the store a minute, my man." Hussein can wait, he's not going to die without his lemon fruit pie.

Sitting on the tall stool behind the register, I'm feeling very important, princely. I dust my counter kingdom with a feather-duster scepter. In walk two boys about my age but bigger, townie kids on their way home from school. I hide the duster quick.

One kid's face is solid freckle. The other is a braceface with a bowl haircut; he reminds me of my archenemy, Greg Garnett. My Lex Luthor. A bad egg.

Last year, after he lit his desk on fire and kicked his sixth-grade teacher (in the nuts, supposedly), he was expelled from Creamery Street Elementary, the school in town, which is where Hussein and I would go if our parents hadn't put us in a one-room school to protect us from the Greg Garnetts of the world. Instead we ended up in one room with him, trapped.

He called Missy Harelik *Missy Harelip,* and she really does have a harelip; bald-headed April-Dawn Purdy was *Purdy Ugly;* and I was *Ahab the Ay-rab.* When I'd tell him my name's not Ahab, and I'm not Arab, I'm from Africa, he'd go *haw, haw,* showing his mouth full of metal and rubber bands. He never messed with Hussein, though. My brother's crutches double as weapons.

I watch these two, not–Greg Garnett and Freckleface, in the fish-eye mirror. They come to the counter with sodas and junk, and Freckleface says, "Hussein. 'Sup." I ring them up, and they seem surprised, like maybe they were expecting something for free.

"I'm not Hussein," I say. "He's my brother."

Not–Greg Garnett gives me a look, like *whatever,* and Freckleface says, "Tell your brother that Joey from Royal Tallow says 'sup." Royal Tallow is a soccer team. It is also the rendering plant. On certain days, an evil wind blows from Royal Tallow. Hussein plays for the Optimist Club; he thinks they sell eyeglasses. "And tell him Joey says Optimists suck."

Whatever.

After Greg Garnett found out we were Siamese, he wouldn't quit needling me about it: *Show me your scars, show me your scars.* That Halloween, Missy Harelik's mom brought a Cabbage Patch Doll to school. An actual head of cabbage, but stuck to the cabbage with toothpicks were pig ears, eyeballs, and a snout. Farm humor, I guess. It wore a bonnet and a dress and attracted flies. *Show me your scars,* said Greg Garnett, shoving the snout in my face.

When I get home I toss the fruit pie to Hussein. I hold up the yellow devil head in its plastic bubble, and my eyes go back and forth from the devil head to my brother. He says, "What're you doing?"

"Nothing."

Just as I thought. Hussein's eyebrows, the slanted eyebrows, give him a devilish look.

Tonight we stay in our separate beds. Hussein sleeps sitting up on pillows. The head injury instruction sheet on the fridge says to keep his head elevated. I don't sleep. Every hour, Mama creeps in and bends her ear to Hussein's mouth, listening for breath. Baba comes home. They fight. *Hospital bill* and *her fault* ping off the kitchen walls.

I wake up late, feeling fuzzy and excited. It's Saturday. I

have a date today at the library. Miss Jones, Kitty Jones; I think she's wow.

In the kitchen this morning there is more fighting. Our father is at work. Our mother tells Hussein no football, which is what she calls soccer. He insists his brain is telling him that it, his brain, is good to go, which makes him sound crazy, not convincing, and Mama says N-O.

He takes a drink of juice. Then he asks can he come to the library with me. Hussein rarely sets his foot in the library, but the sheet on the fridge does say that personality changes are common symptoms of a head injury.

Also taped to the fridge is a newspaper clipping of Hussein in his Optimists uniform with the caption: *a very special soccer player.*

"No football game," says our mother. "You promise."

When Hussein says let's ride the bike, I shrug. I don't always feel like putting on that much of a show.

Our mother says, "No bicycle, not today. No buts."

So we ride the bus.

We get off in front of the fairgrounds, where a carnival is setting up for Dairy Days, or as the banners strung up downtown say, Dairy Daze. Past the fairgrounds a ways, past the rinky-dink mini golf course and the public pool, is the junior high, where—squinting hard—I see a flea circus of tiny blue Optimists doing practice drills on the playing field.

The library is right across the street. We wait for the green light, and Hussein says, "Later, egghead." He's off toward the junior high, crutches flashing in the sun.

Do I go after him, wrestle him to the sidewalk? The light is green. I let him go, what else can I do.

The library smells of old books and new carpet and feet. At the circulation desk, Miss Jones is cutting out construction-paper frogs and tadpoles. "For this," she rolls her eyes and snips the air with her scissors, "I got a master's degree." Then she smiles at me, sort of, more like a lip twitch. But coming from her, it's like getting a gold star.

I used to be a little afraid of Miss Jones and the violent way she pounded her due-date stamp, afraid to ever ask her a question, even though that's what librarians do, they answer questions. Stupid questions, mostly. Like, someone'll slap his hands on the desk and go, *Bridge?* And she's supposed to psychically know whether bridge means author, title, or subject. I was afraid of asking a stupid question, so I didn't talk to her at all.

We never said a word. Until I found *Very Special People* misshelved in Fantasy. Miss Jones frowned at the three-legged man on the book jacket and said, *You can't check this out. You need permission from your parents.*

I said, *But I am one.*

One what? she said.

A very special person.

I had on my prosthetic leg, so I was just an ordinary kid with a limp, and I always came to the library by myself—she couldn't have known I was a twin, let alone Siamese. So I told her.

I kept *Very Special People* under my mattress, partly because my mother might not like it, and partly because of the thrill of having a secret, something all mine. In bed at night beside my brother, I'd tell him stories about Chang and Eng, Daisy and Violet Hilton, the Tocci brothers, and Millie-Christine. I renewed *Very Special People* twice and forgot to a third time, but Miss Jones forgave the late fee. When I did finally return it, she had a new book waiting for me: *We Who Are Not As Others.*

After that came *Anomalies and Curiosities of Medicine,* then *Special Cases.* Miss Jones showed me a photograph of a sculpture on the side of a thousand-year-old church: what is supposedly

Eve coming out of the rib of Adam is obviously Siamese twins—stomach to stomach, two heads, four arms, just two legs. It's us.

Today Miss Jones has a movie for me. She takes me to a closet of a room, where she clips headphones over my ears and plugs me into the TV. She presses PLAY and then leaves me alone in the flickering dark.

Watching this movie, *Freaks,* I get a sort of homesick feeling for the circus life: there's a legless man who walks on his hands and an armless girl who holds a fancy drink with her toes; there's a caterpillar man—no arms, no legs—who rolls a cigarette with his tongue then strikes a match with his teeth; there are midgets, a bearded lady, a half man–half woman, and, yes, yes, Siamese twins!—the Hilton sisters, Daisy and Violet!

It's one thing to see them in photographs, or read their obituary on microfiche, but actually hearing them talk and seeing them *alive* is something else. The sideways way they move, dancing back to back, they're some creature out of a myth. When a clown pinches Daisy's arm, Violet feels it too, and when Violet's boyfriend gives her a kiss, Daisy goes, "Oh!" and gets a dreamy look in her eyes.

Somewhere in all this, there's a story about a trapeze lady, a normal, who marries a midget for his money. At the wedding, a dwarf goes around the tabletop, offering everyone sips from a giant goblet. Everyone is chanting, "Gooble, gobble, we accept her, one of us, one of us."

But when the dwarf holds the drink up to the trapeze lady's lips, she screams, "Freaks! *Freaks!*" and knocks the goblet away.

In the end, after she tries to poison the midget, the freaks do make her one of them. They turn her into a Chicken Woman— covered with feathers and so fake, I laugh out loud.

○

Monday at school we all partner up and outline each other's bodies on butcher paper, then we paint self-portraits. While we're painting, Kathy Harelik, Missy's mom, comes around, measuring our heads; we're doing a song for the Dairy Days festival, and she's sewing us cow hats.

Hussein won't let her near his head. He says, "I'm not putting on some lame cow hat." Instead of fighting it out with him, Kathy Harelik moves on to the next head.

Missy calls my brother a baby, and he says, "Shut your face, Hare*lip*."

"I'm telling," she says. "Mom!"

"Your mom's a dumb bitch," he says. The whole room sucks in its breath and falls silent.

Bitch? Where did *that* come from? That is not a Hussein word. Egghead, yes. Jerk, maybe, but *bitch?*

Kathy Harelik stands over him, her mouth pressed into a line. Hussein glances up at her and says, "Well, you are one." Then he goes back to his painting, la, la, la, like this is a perfectly normal way to behave.

Mrs. O taps his shoulder and marches him outside. When they come back in, he grumps apologies to Missy and her mom.

I ask him, "What did Mrs. O say?"

"She said I can be a cowboy."

After I finish my self-portrait, I go to the sink to wash the paint off my hands. The soap is all red because my brother used it first. Rubbing the bar between my hands, something gives my palm a scratch. No blood, but it stings. I run the soap under the faucet, rinsing off the pink lather; there's a sharp speck. I dig around it with my thumbnail. A needle. Someone stuck a sewing needle in the soap. I wrap the wicked soap in a paper towel and drop it into the trash.

Mrs. Martian, still wearing the neck brace, is on a stepladder, hanging our self-portraits on the wall, while Hussein passes T-pins up to her. April-Dawn has given herself long, long hair. Missy has a neat little heart-shaped mouth. The one-legged monster with horns and fangs is my brother.

That evening we have a tug-of-war over the clicker. Hussein got to watch *Fear Factor* last week; it's my turn for *Antiques Roadshow*. He's stronger. He wins.

So he hit his head, so what? It's *my turn.*

Blocking the TV, I hold up his flower pillow in one hand, scissors in the other. "Give me the clicker."

He turns up the volume.

I put a corner of pillow between the scissor blades.

He cocks his arm, aiming the clicker at my head.

I squeeze the scissors shut. A nose-shaped piece of pillow lands on the floor, along with some sad crumbles of foam. Right then our mother walks in. It's his pillow, but I'm the one who bursts into tears.

Stitching the flower pillow back together, Mama decrees that Hussein will have half of his show, I'll have half of mine. But he complains that he's already watched most of his half, and if he misses the end, he won't know who won.

I volunteer to take the middle half of my show. "That way, Hussein, you'll only miss the part of the game where they eat African spiders or maggoty cheese."

He won't look at me. He's turned to stone.

When I see what's on *Antiques Roadshow*—an old wide chair, wide as a bench, with side-by-side imprints where two people sat—I start hopping up and down, bouncing all around the family room. Before the bow-tie guy tells us, I guess what it is: Eng's chair. I mean, I didn't know whose chair, Chang's or Eng's, but I knew it belonged to one of them.

How can Hussein just sit there sulking under a black cloud like this is nothing big?

Chang and Eng lived in two houses a mile apart. Three days at Chang's house, three days at Eng's, and this chair is the very chair they sat on when they stayed at Eng's.

Later, I wake up thirsty. As I'm getting out of bed, I see a moonlit sparkle in the carpet. The sparkle turns out to be a T-pin, sharp end pricking up. Crawling along the carpet, I find another T-pin, then another, a trail of T-pins from my bed to my side of the dresser, where I keep my crutches. If not for the moon, my foot would be a bleeding pincushion.

You with the evil eyebrows sleeping in my brother's bed— *who are you?*

Ten minutes from now, we're supposed to be onstage at Dairy Days, and Hussein's still in the shower. I play Solitaire, flipping the cards fast. The face cards are all Siamese. Last night he slept next to me in bed. It gave me a bit of a shock this morning when I opened my eyes and there he was.

He comes in cloaked in a towel, like Dracula, and I tell him, "Fathead, get dressed!" And he throws open his towel, revealing the clothes he already has on underneath. Then he falls over from cracking up.

We bungee our crutches to the rack on our bike. We put on our helmets. He sits in front holding the handlebars, and I sit behind holding onto his middle, while his white shoe pumps one pedal, my silver shoe pumps the other. Without him I'd just be some kid with one leg. Together we're something special.

I clinch him tighter and say, "You came back."

He says, "I didn't go anywhere."

"You weren't you. You were Dr. Jekyll and Mr. Hyde."

"I was mad," he says.

"What were you mad at?"

"I don't know," he says, annoyed. "I was just mad." Above downtown, a white balloon floats up and up, shrinking into the sky. "You told everyone, 'Hussein wasn't wearing his seat-belt.' You made me look stupid."

Weaving through the sidewalk sales, we spot the cow hats in the crowd. They're furry cow-print hoods, really, with eye-holes and paper cones glued onto the sides. Mrs. O presents Hussein with a red felt cowboy hat.

We're going on after the Brush Off. Every year our town tries to break its own world record for the most people brushing their teeth at once. After us is the Ugly Dog Contest. So we're in a sandwich of the two most popular events at Dairy Days (what teeth brushing and ugly dogs have to do with dairy, I'll never figure out).

Through my eyeholes, I see someone in a Clo the Cow suit giving out toothbrushes, and there is a funny moment when Clo comes over to all of us little cows. In this moment there is nothing strange about getting a toothbrush from a cow: we're all just cows here.

The cows of Union School lift their hoods, baring their teeth, brushes ready for the gun to go off. I lift my hood and look around for our mother, who's been downtown for hours, shop-ping at sidewalk sales. Our father, like always, is at the store. I can't find Mama through all the tall heads. I see a familiar head, and the familiar head lowers her sunglasses at me. "Hassan?"

Miss Jones!

She says, "Did we miss the dogs?" By *we*, she means herself and the woman with her, who has a gold hoop through the middle of her nose, like a bull, in honor of Dairy Days, perhaps.

I tell her no, the ugly dogs are coming after our song. I point out my brother in his cowboy hat, then I ask, "Are you two sis-ters?" Chang and Eng married sisters.

And Miss Jones says, "Yeah, *sisters*." They look at each other and laugh.

Then, at the gunshot, we start brushing our teeth. We brush hard, as if that'll help break the record, all of us getting red in the face from laughing and brushing so furiously.

We don't set a new world record. Next year.

Climbing the stairs up to the stage, I wonder if our Anonymous Donor is here watching; if I were our Anonymous Donor, I'd want to see what we were up to. We are joined onstage by Mr. Ortiz (father of Bill and Luis) and his mariachi band, in their spangly sombreros and tight pants with silver buttons up the sides. They begin to strum, and we sing, "Oh, give me land, lots of land, under starry skies above. Don't fence me in."

Mrs. O and Mrs. Martian mouth the words along with us. Miss Jones and her sister hold hands and sway.

"Let me be by myself in the evening breeze. And listen to the murmur of the cottonwood trees. Send me off forever, but I ask you please, don't fence me in."

There's Clo, who could be our Anonymous Donor, for all I know—oh! and there's our mother, tiny and smiling. I let go of a crutch and give her a little waist-high wave.

"Let me wander over yonder till I see the mountains rise. I want to ride to the ridge where the West commences. And gaze at the moon till I lose my senses."

The flashbulb is Kathy Harelik.

Blinded, I sing louder, "I can't look at hobbles, and I can't stand fences. Don't fence me in."

There's a hush, then the rain of applause, as I blink the stars out of my eyes. At the bottom of the stairs, hairless and shivering in its owner's arms, is the smallest dog I've ever seen. Our mother is waiting with her shopping bags. She crushes us together in her arms and says, "Good brothers."

The End of Everything

TINA ducks out of the airport men's room. The women's room would've been safer, but she wasn't thinking straight, she is not herself tonight. Concentrating *heel-toe, heel-toe*, she clips in silver pumps, size twelve, down the deserted concourse. Pink polka-dot minidress with a browning white rose pinned over her heart. Her lips, greased with lipstick so pink it shouts, clench an unlit Benson & Hedges Deluxe Ultra Light Menthol 100.

Outside, the air's the same as the air at any airport—airless, turbid with exhaust. The shuttle to the long-term lots is pulling away from the curb. Tina lunges after the shuttle, then hurls her duffel bag at it. The strap catches on the rear bumper. Her sky-blue bag is dragged into the night.

Three cigarettes later, the shuttle comes around, Tina's blackened sky-blue bag still caught on its bumper. The shuttle is skunky, smelling of pot smoke. To Tina's reflection in the fish-eye mirror, the driver says, "What a beautiful smile." Tina is not smiling. "Baby," he says, "your smile just makes my day." At the purple lot, he asks for a hug.

When Tina's pickup won't start, she pounds the dash with

her fists. She turns the key again. The lights light up and flicker, the engine doesn't turn over. Popping the hood, she accidentally pops off a press-on nail.

Headlights spotlight Tina on the purple lot stage, and she gathers herself, juts her hip, makes herself womanish; being a woman alone in a dark parking lot is *less dangerous* than being a man dressed as one. A crown of spinning yellow lights comes on: airport security to the rescue. Tina's a little turned on by this damsel-in-distress scene. That is, until the make-believe no-gun cop gets out of the car: he is wider than he is tall, muscle-bound and squat, and his arms can't touch his sides. *What tiny little shiny shoes he has,* Tina thinks.

Shorty jiggles some wires and shrugs. "Could be your battery, ma'am." He doesn't have jumper cables. He radios roadside assistance, and the action figure he is drives off in his big toy cop car.

Tina looks up at the starless sky and tries to count her blessings. She counts one: that she has come down from the Tweety Bird acid, mostly. Her jaw aches. Her shimmery eyelid spazzes. She thinks, *Seven years sober—pfft.*

The tow guy is wiry, snaggletoothed, baseball-capped. He could be a Rusty or a Curly, except for the gold jewelry: a fat chain around his neck and a huge nugget ring. He looks like rough trade, Tina's type. She's partial to dirt under the fingernails, behind the ears, and a sunburnt neck. His small eyes are flinty and opaque.

"So," Tina bats her lashes. "You gonna give me a jump?"

"Battery's fine." He wipes some parts with a red rag. "Probably your plug wires or moisture in your distributor, can't say for sure. I can give you a tow to my shop, and they'll take a look at it tomorrow."

At the shop, Curly sits at a scarred wooden desk behind a

steel mesh partition, and he puts up his feet, unsettling a heap of cigarette butts. In the waiting area, there are no chairs, just a table arrayed with yellowing catalogs of used cars. Tina hugs her filthy sky-blue bag and asks Curly to call a cab to take her into the city.

He tells her, "There's no cabs here. There's cabs back at the airport."

Tina's voice drops an octave. "We're not at the airport anymore."

"Relax," says Curly, picking up the phone and dialing. "Buddy of mine'll give you a ride." To the phone, he says, "What's doing? Lady here needs a ride to the city."

"How much?" says Tina, pressing her nose against the cool mesh partition.

Curly covers his mouth with his hand, talking too low for Tina to hear. He hangs up and says, "He's playing with the dogs. He'll be right over."

"How much?" she says again.

"Sixty."

Tina points out that a Super Shuttle from the airport only costs twenty dollars, less if you've got a coupon.

"You're not at the airport anymore." Curly winks, she thinks, or maybe it was just a trick of the grim flickery light.

In God we trust, all others pay cash: Tina reads this placard over and over. Her wig itches. The room ticks. She watches the clock. The revolutions of the red minute hand make her dizzy. She can still make it to The Hole in the Wall in time for last call.

A big black car pulls up. Tinted windows, vinyl top. Fancy. The driver, whose middle has settled into the soft, hippy shape of sitting in a driver's seat for so long, holds the back door open for Tina. He actually bows. He pushes his glasses up his nose.

The driver punches the gas and says, "Broke down, huh?

Bet you didn't have to wait long before somebody stopped. You're lucky you're a female aged eighteen to forty, that's why somebody stopped for you so quick. If it'd been me that broke down, I'd've been waiting forever." He speeds through a yellow light and runs a red one. "And you're lucky I was up. I was over at my parents', playing with the dogs. My parents're on a cruise."

Playing with the dogs had sounded euphemistic to Tina when Curly said it.

The driver says, "I love dogs, I just love animals. Heck, I won't even kill an ant. If there's an ant, I'll pick it up in a paper towel and put it outside." Tina's stomach jumps when they lurch up the freeway on-ramp. "I had a lady from QVC in my car once. Quality Value Channel. You know, home shopping. Her dog'd just died. I was telling her about my dog—he's a lab mix, his name's Rudy—and she missed her dog so much, she asked could we go over to my place and play with Rudy. Another time, I was on my way to pick up a guy, and there was this dead dog on the side of the road. So sad, lying there like that in the gutter. What kind of, of *a-hole*, excuse my French, hits a dog and just leaves him there? I couldn't leave him there. Had to at least give him a proper burial. I had to drop out of medical school because I couldn't dissect a dog. My dad was pretty disappointed."

Tina tells herself, *Don't think about dads. Don't think about goddamn disappointed dads.* But, of course, she can't stop thinking about it: her father lit-up and proud of his youngest son, the good son, who is about to be married and make babies, carrying on the family name like good sons do, her father radiant and happier than Tina has ever seen him be, until Tina takes her seat beside him.

The driver says, "You'd think my dad would be glad that I

work for him, you'd think he'd be like, 'Someday, son, all these cars will be yours.' There's only one animal I can't stand and that's snakes."

Oh, for fuck's sake. Can we get more Freudian?

"When I was a kid, me and my sister were out back in the garden, and she's stepping on the freaking flowers. On purpose! Because she knows I'm the one that's gonna be in trouble. So, I pick up the hose, and it's, it's a snake."

The driver is finally silent. Tina says, "What were you going to do with the hose?"

"Spray her! What'd you think? That I was gonna *strangle* her? Ha, ha, ha, ha."

Tina is afraid. She watches herself be afraid, as if watching herself in a dream.

The driver says, "You had little brothers, right? You were always getting them in trouble, right?"

No, I get my stupid, selfish self in trouble. Tina clouts herself a couple times on the head. Then, *Don't think about the wedding. Don't think about ruining your baby brother's wedding. Just. Don't. Think. About. It.* She slides into the seat beside her father. His face falls, crushed. The wedding takes forever to begin: the bride has split her dress. Tina's mother—who upon seeing Tina said simply, *Merde*—has gone off in search of a needle and thread. A colorful snowflake pattern crazes the skin of her father's stricken face.

"I was always in trouble," the driver says, glaring Cotton Mather-ishly at Tina in the rearview mirror. "You know who the worst customers are? Females aged eighteen to forty. You know what I'm talking about. Girls are so much worse than guys. You know what I'm saying."

Tina says, calmly, not wanting the driver to smell her fear, "Take the next exit."

"Look," the driver holds up a fan of golden tickets. "The strip clubs give me these to give out. I get a lot of customers asking where can they get some action."

"Hang a right," says Tina. "Stop up there at the ATM."

"Strippers are the smart ones. These tickets get you in the door, but then you gotta pay for drinks, and drinks are like ten bucks apiece, and then there's tips. Even if it's your birthday, and everyone's there just for you, if you so much as touch *the stage* they throw you out."

They pull into a bus stop in front of the cash machine. Tina tries the door handle. "How do I get out of here?"

The driver pushes a button and Tina's lock jumps up.

She takes eighty out of the cash machine, leaving a balance of $3.29. According to her receipt, it's 0117 o'clock. Just enough time for a drink at The Hole. She throws three twenties at the driver. *No tip for you, scary little man-clown.* She walks away fast, tucking her last twenty into her bra. *Heel-toe, heel-toe.*

She doesn't breathe until she's sure the big black car is not coming after her. It occurs to her that she could've ended up dead, strangled. Hacked to pieces. Ahead, a hooded man slumps against the glass of a closed Chinese take-out place. Tina sees neither the man nor the hand-lettered sign in the window that says *funny taste sparerib 99 cents!* because she is having visions of herself as cuts of meat, while her father's voice booms in her head, *When you're dead, you're dead—that's the end of everything.* The hooded man jitters to life when Tina walks by.

"Ma'am?" he says. "I ran out of gas, ma'am. My wife and baby girl are out on the street tonight, and I—"

Tina says, "If I give you a dollar will you leave me alone?" She unzips the pouch on her duffel bag and digs for change. The sobriety chips on her keychain feel like coins, confusing her fingers, so she takes her keys out. A rainbow of aluminum chips, each stamped *Serenity Now*, awarded for seven drug-free anniversaries. The flip sides read: *To Thine Own Self Be True.*

Fuck serenity, Tina thinks, putting money in the man's shaky hand. She keeps on walking. He is right behind her. He jerks the strap of her duffel bag, hard, toppling her to the sidewalk. Then he shoulders her bag and heads the other way. Tina gets up on her feet and goes after him, keys splayed between the fingers of her fist.

The man says, "Don't follow me, ma'am." He is not walking fast. "I said, don't follow me."

Tina considers her arsenal: her keys, her shoddy press-on nails, her silver heels, the pearl-tipped boutonniere pin. He could have a knife. He could have a gun. *Fuck it. Fuck The Hole.* She breaks the sobriety chips free from her keychain and tosses them, chink, into the gutter. *I'm going home.*

Tina bumps the front door shut with her butt. She pulls off her wig, and she is Jeff. His feet, liberated from high heels, throb as the blood comes back. He washes his face at the kitchen sink. The lather is foundation makeup orange. He splashes with cold water—cold shrinks the pores—and blinks droplets from his lashes. He pulls off the lashes. The window over the sink looks out onto an air shaft, and on the other side of the air shaft is his neighbor's window. The old neighbor kept the blinds drawn. The new neighbor has no blinds. The new neighbor is a dwarf. Under the unkind overhead light, this dwarf, who wears a leather cap and chaps with a harness criss-crossing his child-size but very hairy chest, this tiny angry daddy flogs the rump of a plump pink man, spread-eagled and chained to a huge wooden X.

Jeff unzips and wriggles out of the polka-dot minidress, the bridesmaid's dress his mother wore to her older sister's wedding years before. He undoes his bra, and a pair of balled-up socks fall to the floor, along with his ATM card, a twenty-dollar

bill, and several Ativans pilfered from his mother's stash during the Wedding Weekend.

He swallows two Ativans, putting an end to this night.
*Goodnight parade of strange men. Goodnight LSD and seven years of
sobriety. Goodnight Wedding Weekend. Goodnight Tina.*

For breakfast, Jeff downs Bloody Marys at Sakura's Lounge.
Sakura herself shakes maracas and dances like a drunken,
pickled fairy behind the bar. It is not yet 9 A.M. Jeff expected
more from his first drink in seven years, he expected nectar.
But tomato juice with the antiseptic afterburn of well vodka is
what this tastes like, same as it tasted seven years ago.

A man wearing a collander on his head and a checked-
tablecloth toga has parked himself in front of the tinted window, and Jeff wonders, *Insanity? Or performance art?* Collander
Man twirls a toilet plunger, while the current of Financial Dis-
trict drones in corporate drag eddies around him. *Everything we
consume eventually turns to shit,* Jeff thinks, *which in turn becomes
cinderblocks. Cinderblocks are made from the ash of incinerated
sewage. These barroom walls are full of shit.* He sucks the watery
dregs of his third cocktail through a skinny straw.

Outside, Jeff is feeling very relaxed, floating two or three
feet above the sidewalk. He is sure he really is floating, though
only for about ten seconds or so at a time. Then he nearly col-
lides with a man carrying a brand new baby. The baby has on a
blue hat that comes up in a curlicue, like soft-serve ice cream,
all spangled with charms that tremble in the light, dazzling
Jeff's eyes. For a moment, he is absorbed by the splendid hat,
when a cacophony of car horns blows up from the jammed
intersection and breaks his reverie. He mumbles an apology,
glad he didn't cause the man to drop the baby.

A sandwich board outside a florist's advertises *Ass. bouquets* w/ *Rose,* and Jeff can't decide which image is funnier—an ass bouquet, or the class on ass bouquet arranging taught by a grandmotherly type named Rose. He pulls a red rosebud from a plastic bucket and hurries on without paying.

Past Present Future Past Present Future blinks in pink neon over the doorway of Mad Manya's Mystic Tea Room. Slouched on a futon in the front window is a woman wearing a lime-green pantsuit. She is bent over her journal and doesn't see Jeff until he raps the glass and sings, "Billy Jaaack!" She looks up. Jeff kisses the window and Billy Jack kisses back.

Billy Jack is a real woman whose real name is Billy Jack, named after the hero of her mother's favorite film, *Billy Jack,* about a Native-American Vietnam vet, bigot-hating and peace-loving, but karate-chopping when necessary.

Jeff opens the front door, which creates a powerful wind tunnel. The floor is spread all over with ruffling leaves of wet newspaper. Jeff fights against the vacuum to get the door shut again.

Billy Jack has taken a weeklong vow of silence and has been camping in the window, which is normally reserved for art installations. This week, Billy Jack Goldberg *is* the art installation. She holds her journal open for Jeff to see. It says: CHEF JEFF!! WHAT ARE YOU DOING HERE?!!!

"I came home early." He gestures at the newspapered floor with his rose. "What happened?"

WATER PIPE EXPLODED, Billy Jack writes. FLOOD. HOW WAS THE WEDDING?

"I went as Tina."

HA, HA. HOW WAS THE WEDDING REALLY?

"Really, I went as Tina."

Billy Jack does a pantomime of horror, cringing and showing the whites of her eyes, a silent-film star in peril.

"Actually," Jeff says, "I went as Tina in drag as my mother."
Performance art?—hah! Insanity.

Billy Jack guffaws. Then she claps her hand to her mouth,
genuinely horrorstruck. She writes, LAUGHING DOESN'T
COUNT! I DIDN'T BREAK MY VOW, RIGHT??

"Relax," Jeff says, channeling the tow guy from the night
before. He is not floating anymore and is in no mood to reas-
sure anyone. But he brightens when Andrew comes out of the
kitchen carrying a bus tray steaming with clean dishes.
Andrew is now Drew because there are too many Andrews
(Jeff has to keep reminding himself that the *An* is silent). Drew
wears an apron over a vintage dress, blue with a pattern like
fireworks, and heavy steel-toed boots, elegantly butch. Jeff gets
down on his knees on the wet newspaper and holds out the
rose. "For the birthday girl," he says to Drew, who turned
twenty-seven over the Wedding Weekend.

Drew drops the bus tray onto the counter and comes
bounding toward Jeff, kicking up newspapers, and Jeff notices
that the hoop piercing Drew's neck looks redder and more
infected than usual—some places were not meant to be
pierced—and Drew tackles him in a breathtaking embrace.

Drew says, "So, the wedding!—tell me everything." Then
he sniffs, "You've been drinking."

Jeff pulls away. "How was the Ball Dance?"

Billy Jack writes, CHEF JEFF WENT TO THE WEDDING AS
TINA!! and flaps her journal, but the men ignore her. She tugs
at the heel of her sock, which has rotated to the top of her foot.

"The Ball Dance," Drew says, "was completely cosmic. I'm
still on a total endorphin high." For his twenty-seventh birthday, Drew stitched twenty-seven limes to the skin on his back,
chest, and upper arms, and then he danced the Ball Dance until
each lime had ripped free. He takes his birthday rose and

touches it to Jeff's lips, and Jeff winces inwardly. *Andrew, I mean Drew, is a compulsive flirt. He's a Gemini cocktease. It's never going to happen.*

"Come over tonight," Drew coos, "and watch the video."

"I would love to," Jeff lies. "Listen, my truck's in a shop out by the airport, and I was wondering, if you're not busy later, maybe you could give me a ride."

Drew says, "Sorry, cupcake. My coven's having an emergency meeting. A witch confessed to doing speed right before our Beltane ritual, bringing bad tweaker energy into the sacred space, and we need to process. Then we're having a potluck and watching the Ball Dance video. Could you do a main dish? Something vegan?"

Tightly, Jeff says, "Sure."

"Fantastic!" Drew prances off, his boots torturing the poor wood floor in its damp, flimsy newsprint chemise.

Billy Jack waves her journal: I WISH I HAD A CAR. I'D DRIVE YOU.

Jeff smiles weakly. "You're a peach, Goldberg. Is Manya around?"

IN THE ENCHANTED GARDEN. TANK'S OUT THERE TOO.

Tank is Jeff's ex. After meeting at Alcoholics Anonymous, they were together six years, and then Tank took a flying leap off the wagon. These days Tank is more of a Lawnmower, just a fidgety little slip of a thing. Tank is more than Jeff can bear this morning. He thanks Billy Jack for the heads-up.

She writes, MAYBE I COULD BORROW DREW'S MIATA.

"Fat chance," Jeff says under his breath. "And since when do you have a driver's license?"

I DON'T. BUT IF I HAD A FREE MIATA I'D LET PEOPLE BORROW IT. DREW IS SO SELFISH.

Drew is a kept man. He has a sugar daddy, some jillionaire businessman (married, of course) who lives in Germany or

Japan or someplace. Drew works at Mad Manya's for the fun of it.

Billy Jack writes, WHY DID YOU GO TO THE WEDDING AS TINA???

"Tina in drag as my mother," Jeff corrects. "Tina in the polka-dotted minidress my mother wore to her sister's wedding. Oh, and did I mention I was tripping my balls off on acid?" His laugh is cruel, acidic.

Billy Jack writes in bigger letters, WHY.

Drew fumbles a teapot, and Billy Jack and Jeff both jump at the smash. Drew sings, "Butterfingers!"

Enter Mad Manya, whose real name is Michael, sashaying in through the back of the cafe. His cigarette sports an inch of ash. "Drewcifer, are you breaking my dishes again?" Then, through a veil of exhaled smoke, Manya squints at Jeff and says, "Well, well, well, the plot thins. Thank Goddess you're back—we're running low on blintzes and borscht, and we're flat out of Catherine the Great." Catherine the Great is tuna salad.

Jeff doesn't say he's off-duty until tomorrow. He says, "Manya, I need a teeny favor."

Manya moves like the *Queen Mary*, slow and deliberate, and sails into port behind the counter. He lets out a deep sigh, eternally put-upon, as if the weight of the world is pressing the air out of him. "Oh please, Drew, not the turquoise McCoy—must you always destroy the *good* china? Give it a decent burial, will you?"

Drew sweeps the remains into a dustpan. "Teapot," he says, "we hardly knew ye," then he dumps the shards into the trash.

Jeff joins them at the counter. He leans forward on his elbows, making himself smaller, hoping that his request will come across accordingly small. "Manya, my truck's in the shop and—"

"That reminds me, Jeffrey," Manya says, though Jeff's full name is Jefferson. "I need you to do a produce run."

"My truck's in the shop," Jeff says again, louder.

"Whoo, you've been hitting the sauce pretty hard." Manya fans the air in front of his face with his cigarette hand, fanning two precarious inches of ash over the condiment bins. Drew chases Manya's cigarette with the dustpan. Too late. A caterpillar of ash lands in the sour cream. Manya is oblivious.

Jeff shields his vodka-breath with his hand. He says, "No truck—no produce runs. I have bupkes in the bank. Mother may I have an advance? Please?"

Manya sighs as if punctured and tamps out his cigarette in a teacup. Drew spoons the ash out of the sour cream. The front door opens, and a sobering blast rips through the cafe.

A baby-faced woman with a faded, chlorine-green mohawk asks if she can put up a flyer in the window, a homemade wanted poster. Gay gunman on a spree. Billy Jack lifts a corner of her futon so Babyface can get by. Babyface bites off a piece of tape and says, "He shot a man in Michigan and bashed in his face with a hammer, and now three more men are dead—one in Chicago, two in L.A." She slaps the poster onto the window, and the light comes through, illuminating the crude, cartoony sketch of a square-jawed man with dark hair and small, round spectacles. *Cute,* Jeff thinks. *In a preppy sort of way.* On her way out, Babyface says, "Be safe."

Drew says, eyerolling, "What a warm fuzzy ray of sunshine she was."

Jeff begins clearing the newspaper off the floor. Some of it has become papier-mâché, glued on. Billy Jack gets up to help. Drew makes a soymilk latte for himself. Manya claps his forehead and cries, "Jeffrey! You haven't said a word about the wedding—did Tina outshine the bride?"

Billy Jack is aghast. She mouths at Manya, *You knew?*

○

Was it just last week that Jeff sat in the Enchanted Garden telling about the time his mother went to her sister's wedding on acid? Rain pelted a midget, headless statue of David rising like Venus out of the koi pond (no koi, only coins and wishes; some fish went belly-up, some went into the bellies of neighborhood cats). Jeff, Drew, Manya, and a couple Mad Manya's characters—Hunter and Paisley—were kept dry by a blue fairground canopy. Drew shared a helpful hint he picked up as a young rent boy: Chloraseptic sore throat spray, it numbs the gag reflex, and it came in quite handy when he was hired to fellate an entire Elks' Lodge. To top that, Hunter—who paints portraits of drag queens, using makeup as his medium—told a story about shoe-shopping with Vyvyan Vermyn, a seven-foot-tall crossdressing nosferatu: when they came out of the big and wide shoe store, a passerby called Vyvyan a freak, so Vyvyan went after him, pinned him down, and with a long black fingernail deftly popped the guy's eye out of its socket. Jeff got giddily into the spirit, and though he could think of no thrilling anecdote of his own, he did have the one about his mother.

When Jeff's nineteen-year-old mother, Linda Fish, moved in with his father, Jefferson Temple Sr., her parents called her a slut. His mother married his father, and her parents disowned her—how dare she marry some no-goodnik longhair they never even met? Linda's older sister, meanwhile, was engaged to a doctor, who had famously introduced himself to her folks by doing a pirouette and announcing, *Here I am!*

Jeff's mother put a hit of windowpane on her tongue before the ceremony. The long march down the aisle was like: *Linda Temple nee Fish—this is your life!* And during the ceremony, when she burst out laughing at the idea of her sister, a Fish, marrying Dr. Salmon, she convinced herself that everyone would think she was crying. After the kiss, she made a beeline for the bathroom to wipe away her mascara tears, but the more she tried to fix her makeup, the more it smeared. In all of the wedding photos, Jeff's mother is wearing sunglasses. In her parents' copies of the wedding photos, Linda has been airbrushed out.

Jeff said he used to play dress-up in the pink polka-dot bridesmaid's dress. He promised to retrieve it from his parents' attic over the Wedding Weekend and bring it back for everyone to see. Manya half-joked that Jeff should wear the dress to the wedding.

And Drew said, "Ooh, going in drag as your mom—that'd be so *meta!*"

An angular woman with large geometric jewelry came to the back doorway. She was unsoftened by the blur of rain. "Does anybody work here?" she said sharply. "Would it be possible to get an eggplant sandwich?"

Paisley gave the woman his stock dreamy smile, showing off his dimples, and said, "I'll be with you in just a sec, hon." He made no move to arise and follow her inside.

"I could go to the wedding as Tina," Jeff said tentatively, trying it on for size. "Tina could wear the dress." Lightning flash, followed by crashing thunder.

"Tina! Tina!" everyone chanted.

Jeff was jazzed, electric.

Manya said, "Tina will be the belle of the ball!"

"She'll be the belle *with* the balls," Drew quipped.

Did Tina outshine the bride? On his hands and knees, Jeff ponders this as he works at a stubborn, stuck-on strip of newsprint with his thumbnail, which is gummy with press-on nail stickum. *Would a birthday party clown at a funeral outshine the deceased?* Manya and Drew are waiting for an answer.

"Well, she certainly made it memorable," Jeff concedes.

"Who made what memorable? You got a cigarette?"

Jeff is face-to-feet with a pair of Converse low-tops. Tank's. Jeff wants to put his hand on Tank's foot to still the toe-tapping. Tank is a wet cat of his former self; his solidity, his girth, his rocklike steadiness and resolve—it was all puff.

Jeff stands up and the room swims. He takes a deep breath. "Yesterday, my brother, Beau, got married, and I went to the wedding *in drag*. Tina made it an occasion to remember."

"Cool," Tank says through gritted teeth. "Tell him I said congrats, babe. Can I have a cigarette?"

Jeff shakes a cigarette out of his pack. Tank asks for another one for later. He tucks the extra cigarette behind his ear and heads for the door. *Come back*, Jeff dumbly pleads. *Stay and I'll make bread pudding for you.*

Tank is a tic-a-thon, doing the crack dance. Go-going. Gone. *Bye, Tank. We hardly knew ye.*

When Jeff's mother asked if he was bringing *Truck* to the wedding, Jeff didn't bother to correct her, nor did he mention the breakup. Six years and she didn't even know Tank's name. Beau had only known his fiancée, Amy, for six months.

Billy Jack pouts sympathetically at Jeff. "Quit it," he snaps. "You look like a fucking mime." He makes a mean sad-clown face and offers Billy Jack an imaginary flower, and she recoils as if the flower burned her.

"Jeffrey," Manya says. "Let's make a deal. Swear you'll go to a meeting tonight, and I'll give you the advance."

"Deal."

Manya writes a check and tears it out of the ledger. Jeff reaches for the check, and Manya snatches it away. "Cross your heart," he says.

"Hope to die, stick a needle in my eye." Jeff pockets the

check and turns to leave. He intends to cash the check, then have another cocktail or two or three. He opens the door and Rita Rockit breezes in; she is the evil wind that blows from the east; she is a demon disguised as a beautiful woman; at night, she stars in a one-woman show about Lizzie Borden, *Lizzie!* with songs such as "Ax Me If I Care"; by day, she reads Tarot cards at Mad Manya's. She presses herself against Jeff, envelops him, wraps him in Rita.

"Chef Jeff, my love," she breathes in his ear. "Marry me."

Jeff's face goes hot.

"Seriously," Rita says, "have you ever considered a relationship with a woman? Can I be your Plan B?"

Flustered, Jeff says, "But I'm gay as a"—his voice cracks— "*goose*. And right now I can't think past getting my truck fixed and getting it home from the boondocks."

Rita gives him a penetrating look. "I think you can't think past your next drink." Jeff's jaw drops and she says, "It's not psychic, silly goose. I can smell the alcohol coming out of your pores. Where's your truck at?"

"Past the airport."

"I'll be your chariot, no problem."

Jeff says, "My angel."

Swing low, sweet chariot, he sings to himself all the way to the liquor store. *Coming for to carry me home.*

Night has fallen by the time Jeff's parking fairies find him a space several blocks from his building. The broken-down pickup was the cherry on the cake of the Wedding Weekend, a cruel epilogue, but now—three hundred dollars and a new timing belt later—the farce is over, *fin.*

Cradling a box of wine and walking lightly, almost skipping,

Jeff laughs out loud at something Rita told him during the drive to the mechanic: she dreamed she was on a TV show in which she had to perch on a high platform, sing her favorite song, and then plunge to her death. The show was called *Swan Song*. She'd begun a few bars of "Is That All There Is?" and stopped, deciding it was too glib. Instead she sang "Shuffle Off to Buffalo," doing a soft-shoe, then she shuffled off the platform, shuffling off her mortal coil. It had been her childhood bedtime song.

Jeff never had a bedtime song, though he did have a childhood drinking song: *Chevaliers de la Table Ronde, goutons voir si le vin est bon. Goutons voir, oui, oui, oui. Goutons voir, non, non, non. Goutons voir si le vin est bon.*

Children drank wine in France, and so did Jeff, in America, starting around age six. Later, he would sing this song with the French Club in high school, hoisting a paper cup of grape juice, and the nonsense sounds he'd sung with his mother became words: *Knights of the Round Table, let's taste to see if the wine is good. Let's taste, yes, yes, yes. Let's taste, no, no, no. Let's taste to see if the wine is good.* As the song went on, the verses turned darker: *On my tombstone I'd like written, Here Lies the King of the Drinkers. The moral of this story is to drink before you die.*

He told Rita about "Chevaliers de la Table Ronde," or as he has come to think of it, "The Drink Yourself to Death Song." When she asked what his swan song would be, he said, "My Way," which was a lie. The truth, too embarrassing to admit: "You Light Up My Life."

A streetlight gutters out when Jeff passes beneath it. He quickens his pace, the way horses do when they're headed back to the stable. What's the hurry? There will be no waiting lover, no long hot bath, no curling under the duvet watching bad TV, because he still has to cook for Drew's vegan Ball Dance video potluck, and he promised Manya he'd go to AA. Jeff hurries anyway. Inside his building, he takes the stairs two at a time, and when he gets to his floor he is breathless, wheezing.

First thing, he fires up a cigarette. He opens the fridge. Cooking for a living, he rarely cooks for himself, so the fridge is inhospitably bare, aside from an eclectic mix of condiments—capers, lemon curd, Vietnamese hot chili sauce—and, in the crisper, furry red bell peppers and liquefying spinach. Something is balled in tin foil. Goat cheese, Jeff guesses from the smell, or some other soft cheese past its sell-by date. He flicks a short curly hair out of an egg cup in the refrigerator door. With phyllo dough dug out of the freezer frost and a half-stick of crumby butter, Jeff will make do.

Vegan shmegan, he thinks, brushing each leaf of phyllo with melted butter. Buzzed on box wine and humming along to Julie Andrews, he spoons mystery cheese into his turnovers.

Across the air shaft, the dwarf next door pinches clothespins onto a man shackled to the X, a different man than the one last night. This one is much thinner and grayer and splotched with purple lesions. He has tubes up his nose and breathes from an oxygen tank. Clothespin fronds fan out from the man's thighs and stomach, as high as the dwarf can reach.

At Drew's, Jeff sets his turnovers on a table among the lentil loaves and lentil stews. He tries to guess which witch is the bad witch based on whose eyes are the reddest and puffiest. Everyone but unflappable Drew is equally red-eyed. Jeff feels galumphing in the company of these weepy Wiccans, miserably prodding their plates of lentils.

On TV, Drew shimmies and shakes his limes. In person, he has on a tank top that flaunts his Ball Dance scabs. He nibbles a turnover. "Yum, what's in this?"

"Soy cheese," Jeff says. "Capers. Spinach. Roasted red peppers."

"Everybody watch! I'm about to lose another lime!" Drew says. Except for Jeff, everybody here now is on the sidelines in the video, watching Drew dance in the flesh and dodging the occasional lime. The limes aren't exactly flying—one or two every few minutes.

"So," Jeff says, "how long did it take for all twenty-seven limes to come off?"

Drew says, "Three hours."

"Oh shoot, I wish I didn't have to go. I promised Manya I'd go to a meeting."

Jeff bids good-bye to the witches, and the witches say, "Blessed be."

Gay AA still meets in the same basement room of the GLBTQ Community Center. Jeff remembers when the letter T for transgendered was added; the Q is news to him—*Queer? Queen? Quiche-eater?* The meeting has already begun. He arrives during the moment of silence. On the wall, there is the same mural of bulbous female shapes in various shades of purple. And the room smells the same, musty and mothbally and oddly savory, the way instant mashed potatoes taste.

Instead of praying, Jeff is thinking back to the first time Tank walked in through that door. Tank was not an alcoholic, he was a drug addict, a defector from Narcotics Anonymous. *There's no talk of serenity in NA,* Tank told Jeff over coffee and cookies at the end of the meeting. *There's no spirituality. NA is hardcore—it's about just staying alive.*

Jeff had been brought up agnostic, and after a year of sobriety, he was still grappling with Step Three of the Twelve Steps: surrender to a Higher Power, deciding to turn his will and life over to God. The word *God* made him wiggly. Then along came Tank. Tank had *faith,* he was overflowing with it.

"Now," says the meeting secretary, a member of a troupe of

drag queens who dress as nuns, "we'll recite the Serenity Prayer."

"Goddess grant me," everyone but Jeff says, "the power of water, to accept with grace the things I cannot change."

Goddess? Power of water?—what the fuck happened to "God grant me the serenity"?

"The power of fire," they say, "for the courage to change the things I can. The power of air, for the wisdom to know the difference. And the power of earth, for the strength to continue on my path."

As much as Jeff was always troubled by the *God grant me* aspect of the Serenity Prayer—like *under God* in the Pledge of Allegiance, which Jeff's father had instructed him never to say—he found comfort in the ritual. Instead of turning his will and life over to the Goddess, Jeff decides that he's fulfilled his promise to Manya, he came to a meeting, and now he's going to get drunk. Drun*ker*.

At The Hole in the Wall, someone has written above the jukebox: *Music is the only Higher Power.* And underneath that: *one Song at a time.* "Any requests?" Jeff calls to Billy Jack, who's seated on a throne known as the Blowjob Chair, which is rightfully hers, she'd say if she were speaking; she'd say, *My initials are B. J. after all.* She's working on a book of crossword puzzles, naked except for knee-high red boots. Not looking up from her puzzle, she shakes her head no.

Jeff fits a quarter into the slot and punches F66, the buttons for Vyvyan Vermyn's raucous, ironic cover of "You Light Up My Life."

Gin and wine, you'll be fine loops through Jeff's mind. He orders a gin and tonic. His song starts up, and he asks Billy Jack to dance. She shakes her head vigorously no.

"Come on," he says. "I'm sorry I bit your head off earlier.

I'm sorry I called you a mime. Dance with me, please?" He grabs her red-booted leg and tries to pull her out of the Blowjob Chair. She whaps him with her crossword puzzle book.

Jeff slamdances alone. Vyvyan screams, "So many dreams I kept deep inside me! Alone in the dark but now you've come along! And you light up my li-i-ife!"

When the song ends, Jeff orders another gin and tonic. He sneaks a maraschino cherry when the bartender's back is turned. The cherry flavor transports Jeff: he is five, drinking a Shirley Temple. Before Linda became French, before wine with dinner and whenever Linda didn't feel like drinking alone, and before it became apparent that boys were supposed to drink a Roy Rogers, there were Shirley Temples. And Jeff was sure that Shirley Temple, the movie star, had to be related because they shared the same last name; he thought all Washingtons were descended from George.

He goes over to Billy Jack and presents her with a cherry-stem knot he tied with his tongue. "I really am sorry I was a jerk to you," he says. She opens her arms for a hug, and he hugs her stiffly, keeping his distance from her naked body. He says, "Why are you naked?"

In the margin of her crossword puzzle book she writes, WHY DID YOU GO TO THE WEDDING IN DRAG???

"Why did you take your vow of silence?"

BECAUSE I'M SICK OF MY SHTICK.

"Everyone loves your shtick, Billy Jack. You're hilarious."

I WANTED TO KNOW WOULD PEOPLE LIKE ME IF I WASN'T BEING THE FUNNY JEW. WOULD I LIKE MYSELF. Then she points to WHY DID YOU GO TO THE WEDDING IN DRAG??? and draws a circle around the word WHY.

"I don't know," he says. "Maybe I wanted to leave myself behind. You and everyone else at Mad Manya's are born performers, you're all so *fabulous,* while I'm just the cook. I'm Chef Jeff—whoop de doo."

I CAN'T STOP PERFORMING!! I'M A CLOWN.

"Funny you should bring up clowns." Jeff lights a cigarette and blows smoke out of the side of his mouth. "Not ha ha funny, just interesting."

Billy Jack puts two fingers to her lips, asking for a cigarette.

"They're menthol," Jeff says, and Billy Jack waves never mind. "You know the polka-dotted dress I wore to the wedding? My mother's minidress? It was my clown outfit when I was little. So one day, I'm six, I'm in my clown outfit, and I'm playing with the salad spinner, and my mother says, 'Shh! You must be very quiet or the soufflé will fall.'" Jeff imitates his mother's French accent. "She tells me, 'It's a beautiful day. Go outside and *jouer.*'"

A cheese soufflé was baking, Jefferson Sr. napped on the sofa, and baby Beau lay in his playpen, teething a ring of plastic keys. The salad spinner whirred faster, faster, faster, until Linda made it stop. She whispered, "Go outside and *jouer.*" Jeff tiptoed to the back door. After closing it gently behind him, he shot off running. Around and around the willow tree, then he tripped on the hem of his clown outfit and fell face-first in the dirt.

Jeff lifted his head, spitting out grit. He wanted to yell, but he had to be very quiet or the soufflé would fall. He sat up and brushed the dirt off his clown outfit. A thin sunbeam shined on something red and green nestled in a crook of willow root. A hummingbird, dead.

Jeff had never seen a hummingbird be still. It weighed nothing in his hand. He turned his hand in the light, making the feathers go red, green, red, green.

Marching slowly, Jeff led a solitary funeral procession back to the house. "Shh!" his mother said, shooing him out of the kitchen. "The soufflé!" The funeral march continued into the living room, where his father was humped on the sofa, sound asleep.

Jeff shook his father's shoulder, and his father stirred but didn't wake. Jeff shook it harder, and his father bolted upright, murder in his eyes. "Look," Jeff said, holding out the hummingbird. "It's an angel."

"There's no such thing as angels," his father scoffed. "When you're dead, you're dead—that's the end of everything."

Jeff says to Billy Jack, "If there were no angels, then there was no Santa, no Easter Bunny, no Tooth Fairy. Poof!—all gone. And my mother wasn't really French. Her Frenchness wasn't a game. My mother was *gone*."

By now, Billy Jack has filled up her margins, so she flips to the inside cover of her crossword puzzle book: WHEN DID YOUR MOM START ACTING FRENCH?

"You mean, when did she go freaking insane?" Jeff lights his third cigarette in a row. "When my brother Beau was born. I remember her being in bed for a month, crying and crying. Then she snaps out of it, and—*voila!*—she's *Leen-da*. Mom is *Maman*." His drink is only melted ice. He asks Billy Jack if he can get her anything from the bar.

COFFEE. BLONDE WITH TWO SUGARS.

When Jeff returns with their drinks, he says, "My mother's an alcoholic, though she'd tell you she's a *wine connoisseur*." He laughs bitterly. "Well, aren't I a chatty Cathy? *Je suis une* chatty Cathy *ce soir*."

NO NO NO. I'M SO HAPPY YOU'RE OPENING UP TO ME. She makes all the O's into smiley faces for emphasis.

"I never told anyone about the hummingbird before. You know what else? Even after my dad said what he said about when you're dead, you're dead, I still had one small sacred place." Jeff pinches his thumb and pointer together to show Billy Jack how small. "A music box, a crappy Made-in-Taiwan music box. It played 'You Light Up My Life,' and it had a mirror painted with a couple-on-the-beach-at-sunset scene, and this magnetic seagull, a little fridge magnet seagull, that flew in a figure eight. There must've been another magnet behind the mirror that made the seagull move, but when I was a kid it was magic."

I HAD A MUSIC BOX TOO. MINE PLAYED THE THEME FROM THE GODFATHER.

Jeff says, "Over the weekend, I was up in my parents' attic looking for the polka-dotted dress. I found my music box." Billy Jack raises her hand to give him a high-five. He responds with a limp swat. "I had it in my duffel bag last night. And then I motherfucking got mugged."

MOTHERFUCKER, Billy Jack concurs. DID YOU GET HURT??

"No," Jeff says. "For a mugger, he was very polite. He called me ma'am."

Billy Jack giggles at this, then she writes, SORRY! I DIDN'T MEAN TO LAUGH AT YOUR MISFORTUNE.

Jeff smoothes Billy Jack's hair and says, "Don't let me drink any more gin and tonics, okay?"

WANT TO GO?

"I think so."

WANT TO SHARE A CAB?

He'll walk, he says, and helps Billy Jack into her velvet coat. "Why *are* you naked?"

She writes, WHY NOT?

Very gentlemanly, Jeff hails her a cab. He smooches her on the cheek and says, *"Merci beaucoup* for letting me spill my guts. Goodnight, Goldberg." Alone in the empty street, he mutters, "Gin and wine, you'll be fine—*my ass*."

Close to home, he passes the dark arches of the defunct College of Mortuary Science; they mislaid a body, and the lawsuit put them out of business. Then there is an arm wrenched around Jeff's neck, and a faraway voice says, "Don't hurt me," and—*crack!*—Jeff is facedown flat on the sidewalk, a knee jammed into his back. He is too stunned to struggle. Hands dig through his pockets. The knee lets up, and he doesn't move. The slap-slap of running feet grows faint and disappears.

When Jeff comes to and pushes himself up, he feels a crunching under the heels of his hands. Glass. All around him, broken glass sparkles in the streetlight. It takes him a moment to make sense of what just happened; he only heard the sound of the bottle hitting his head, he felt nothing, as if it happened to someone else.

Jeff sprints the rest of the way home.

He stands over the kitchen sink, picking glass out of his palms. The lights are off at the dwarf's next door. Jeff goes into the bathroom and switches on the light. In the mirror, his forehead is huge, skinned pink where the bottle hit. He steps out of his jeans, torn at the knees from the hard fall to the pavement, and turns on the shower. The warm water stings. He wants to cry but can't.

Jeff wraps himself in a voluminous bathrobe that was Tank's. Then he goes to the phone and dials his childhood phone number. His mother answers, "*Allo?*" Her voice is panicky. "*Allo? Allo?*"

"It's me, *Maman*."

"*Mon fils*," she says flatly. "It's the middle of the night. I'm sleeping."

Jeff whispers, "I'm sorry."

"You call in the middle of the night when it's an emergency. You call when someone is dead," she says.

"I called to say I'm sorry. I'm sorry about the wedding. It was supposed to be a joke."

"Oh, so you think it's a joke to ridicule your *mère?* You think it's a joke to break the heart of your *pauvre père?*"

Jeff tenses and says, "That's exactly the same thing your parents said when you married Dad—you broke their hearts. You're such a hypocrite! Not once in six years have you ever asked about my boyfriend, you don't know when his birthday is, you don't even know his name!"

"Truck?"

"His name is Tank!"

Linda says, "I invited him to the wedding."

"You invited *Truck!* And, anyway, we split up, but you wouldn't know that because you never ask me anything."

"Well," she says, "you never tell me anything. Hold on, *s'il te plait.* I'm going to get on the phone in the kitchen." When Linda picks up again, she says, "Maybe you came to the wedding *comme ça* because you wish to live your life as *une femme.*"

"I do not want to become a woman." Jeff plucks at the impossibly twisted phone cord. He hears a slam and some clatter. "What's that noise? What're you doing?"

"Making a *muffin anglaise.*"

"Listen. I didn't call to fight. I didn't mean to ridicule you. If anything, *Maman,* I wanted to feel what it felt like to *be* you, to feel some part of you before you turned—" Jeff cuts himself off.

"Before I turned what? *Qu'est-ce que c'est?* What are you trying to say?"

"Nothing. Forget it. Just tell Dad I'm sorry. And when Beau and Amy get back from their honeymoon, tell them I'm sorry, too."

"They were sad you didn't stay for the reception," she says. "Everyone was asking, 'Where's Cousin Tina?'"

"I was on acid and everyone's faces were melting. It was a horror show. I couldn't stay."

Acid hadn't been part of Jeff's plan. But on the morning of the day he flew home for the wedding, a hippie kicking a Hacky Sack offered acid for sale, and it seemed like kismet. *This is not my addiction,* Jeff told himself, staring at the tiny square of paper stamped with the macrocephalic head of Tweety Bird. *I'm tuning in, not dropping out.*

His mother says, "I sewed up Amy's dress so tight, Beau had to cut her out of it with a steak knife."

"That must've been sexy."

"Sexy for some people, not for them." Then, *"Zut!* My *muffin* is burning! Bye-bye."

Click, dial tone.

The next day at Mad Manya's, Jeff is cheffing up a storm; in addition to the staples—borscht, blintzes, tuna salad—he is preparing *zakuski,* or Russian snacks, for tonight's full moon Mad Tea Soiree: lamb pastries, latkes, pumpkin piroshki, and eggplant caviar with pumpernickel toast points.

He is mincing garlic when hips swish up against his backside, and Rita Rockit's perfume overwhelms the garlic smell. Jeff turns around, and Rita says, "Oh, my God! What happened to you?" The blow to his head has given him a pair of shiners, a crimson half-moon underneath each eye.

"I got mugged," he says.

"Oh, honey," she says. "Were you drunk?"

"Little bit."

Kevin, who comes by with his shopping cart to collect

bottles and cans, pokes his head into the kitchen. He has a jack-o'-lantern grin, no front teeth, just two little fang nubs.

Jeff says, "Hey, Kev. Recycling's out back."

"Thank you and good day, Mr. Jeff." Kevin tips an imaginary hat. "And good day to you, pretty lady," he says, tipping his hat at Rita.

Rita tells Jeff, "When you're not busy, you're coming to me for a Tarot reading."

Later on, when the *zakuski* are done, Jeff is relieved to see a line of people waiting to get readings from Rita; he'd rather not have his fortune told. But when he tries to make his getaway, Rita stops him. "Where do you think you're going, sweetcheeks?"

"Home," he says, "to get dolled up for the party."

"I don't think so," she says. "Sit."

"But you've got customers waiting."

"It won't kill them to wait a little longer."

"I don't have any silver," he says. "You're always supposed to cross a gypsy's palm with silver."

"My treat," she says and hands him her deck. Jeff shuffles awkwardly, the Tarot cards too large to handle. Then Rita deals, turning over the Moon, the Seven of Cups, and the Devil. "Sometimes," she says, "we need to let things fall apart a little, and there can be an amazing burst of creativity. But that's not what I see here." She taps the Moon and the Devil. "You're treating yourself like shit."

She flips another card, Temperance.

"I get it," Jeff says. "Drink less."

She turns over the Tower, then Death.

"Straight up," she says, "If you keep going the way you're going, you're going to die."

Jeff says, "I thought the Death card meant, like, transformation."

"And sometimes Death is just death." Rita takes a pen out of her purse and draws squiggles on a napkin. "This is your name in Sanskrit."

"Jeff?"

"*Devalaya*," she says. "The word for temple. Literally, it means 'house of God.' Get it tattooed over your heart, and when anyone asks you what it means, point to yourself and say, 'Temple.'"

"Why Sanskrit?" says Jeff. "Why not Chinese or Japanese?"

"Because I don't know Chinese or Japanese, I know Sanskrit." Then she turns over the Magician, who has an infinity symbol, a figure eight, floating above his head. "This is you," Rita says. "This is who you are when you're not afraid."

With that, she sweeps the Tarot cards into a pile.

In an effort to be a better drag queen, Jeff is executing his first-ever *tuck*. The art of *tucking* entails stuffing the testicles up inside, stretching the penis back between the buttocks, and taping the flattened package into place. With his crotch trussed in duct tape, Jeff is as neuter as a Ken doll.

He winds more duct tape around his waist, cinching it tight, then zips himself into the polka-dot minidress. He applies concealer to the bruises under his eyes and paints on a bright pink mouth. He teases his wig. Last thing before leaving, Tina drops a steak knife into her faux-leopard handbag.

Halfway to the cafe, Tina hears footsteps behind her, close. She thinks, *Not again*. Heart banging, she unsnaps her handbag and grips the knife. She spins around, chopping the air with her knife, and shouts, "You picked the wrong person to fuck with tonight!" Then she sees who it is. "Oh. Kevin. You scared me."

"Not as much as you scared me, pretty lady," Kevin says,

panting. "Almost gave me a heart attack. You want to get high? You smoke crack?"

They crouch in someone's doorway. Kevin packs what looks like a chunk of rock salt into the end of a glass stem. *This will be a night of firsts,* Tina thinks. *First tuck, first time smoking crack.* She nervously takes a hit; it gives off a sweet, almost fruity, chemical smell. She shuts her eyes, and her anatomy comes into sharp relief, all the red and blue lines squiggling along. *Wah, wah, wah* echoing in her skull. She has to stand up. No, sit. It's too much, she's a bundle of red and blue wires, spraying sparks, and for a glorious moment she is invincible. And then Kevin's hand is on her thigh, sliding up under the hem of her dress.

Tina plops his hand onto the doorstep. "Kevin," she says. "It's me, Jeff."

Kevin says, "You're a very pretty lady, Mr. Jeff," and puts his hand back on her thigh.

There's rough trade, and then there's Kevin. Kevin has two teeth. Tina springs to her feet and hurries on to Mad Manya's. *Heel-toe, heel-toe, heel-toe.*

The cafe is aglow with colored Christmas bulbs twinkling in the chandeliers. *Madame Butterfly* trills out of the stereo. Paisley, shirtless and brilliant with body glitter, alights from table to table, serving snacks and tea; this strikes Tina as grossly unsanitary. The tea-drinkers dart their eyes away when Tina catches them staring at her.

In the Enchanted Garden, a woman is belly-dancing on upturned goblets and eating fire. Drew, poured into distinctly un-vegan leather pants, mimics the belly dancer's snaky undulations. Manya wears a candy-apple-red bouffant and a caftan aswirl with hearts, clubs, diamonds, and spades; and Manya has a single missile of a breast because she was mutated in

Chernobyl, the story goes. Rita Rockit is prim in her Lizzie Borden costume, a blue, blood-spattered Victorian dress. And Billy Jack sits on an old church pew, resplendent in gold lamé and a lavender wig. Tina perches beside her and says, "Kevin the recycling guy just made a pass at me."

Billy Jack writes, EVERYONE GETS LONELY.

"What are you insinuating?" Tina says. "That I'm an asshole? Well, fuck you." She stamps inside, where she is nearly run over by a pair of roller-skating mice in flowered dresses. Vyvyan Vermyn stalks through the front door, insectile in a vinyl cape and corset, leading the artist Hunter along on a leash.

Tina gets a ripe whiff of garbage. The bus tray is stacked high with dishes and leaning towers of teacups. She hefts the bus tray, and her arms are rubbery, uncoordinated. She is sweating profusely.

Tina is taking her pulse when Drew comes into the kitchen. "Feel my pants," he says. She does, and his leather pants have a pulse. She yanks her hand away. "They're couture," he brags. "Zanzare."

Tina says, "Would you tell Paisley to take out the goddamn garbage? It stinks."

"Somebody's on the rag," Drew says.

Rita steps in and says, "Lizzie Borden was on the rag, you know." She lifts her bloody skirts, showing some leg. "She didn't hack her parents to death. Really, she was just having a heavy period."

"Ew!" Drew says, plugging his ears. "La, la, la, I'm not listening."

"Period, period!" Rita taunts him. "Tampax, Kotex, Stayfree!"

Tina says through her teeth, "There are too many people in this kitchen."

Then Manya's enormous breast, followed by Manya, crowds into the kitchen. "Tina, darling, why are you doing dishes? Let Paisley do his job. Is this the dress you wore to the wedding? What's that awful smell?"

"Garbage," Tina says. She squeezes past them and goes behind the counter, where she pulls the garbage out of its pail, then hauls it to the dumpster.

When Tina comes back inside, Manya is unrolling a giant bolt of bubble wrap down the length of the cafe. Tina returns to the dishes. She hoses them off and soaps each one by hand, instead of using the dishwasher. She washes each teacup, plate, and piece of flatware until it squeaks. Hot water loosens the stickum of her press-on nails, and they all fall off and whirl around the drain.

A conga line parades past the kitchen, stomping on the carpet of bubble wrap. It sounds like thunderous applause. Everyone, even the wasp that is Vyvyan Vermyn, goes stomping by, laughing and shrieking and urging Tina to join them. But she can't.

Jeff wakes up after less than three hours of sleep. His mother's Ativan is the only reason he got any sleep at all. He pulls on pants and a sweatshirt and walks out into the too-rosy morning.

At Mad Manya's, Billy Jack is curled up asleep in the front window. Manya will be here any minute to open the cafe for the A.M. coffee rush. Jeff turns his key slowly, until the dead-bolt snicks. He creeps through the cafe. In the Enchanted Garden, he kneels beside the koi pond and pushes his sleeve up to his elbow. He reaches into the water and sifts through the slippery coins. It turns out that people like to make wishes with

Canadian coins, but there are plenty of American coins as well, even a Susan B. Anthony silver dollar.

Jeff doesn't realize someone has come up behind him until he sees the rippled reflection of Billy Jack bowing over him. He freezes.

She goes inside, then comes out again with her journal. I'LL GIVE YOU MONEY, she writes.

He says, "You know I'm just going to buy booze with it."

BETTER YOU BUY BOOZE WITH MY MONEY THAN MONEY PEOPLE MADE WISHES ON.

Jeff lets the coins drop into the water.

Billy Jack gives him eighteen ones and some change, and he asks if there's anything he can do in return. She writes, WILL YOU MAKE ME BAGELS AND LOX?

"Poof, you're bagels and lox!" Jeff rolls his eyes at himself. He spreads a bagel with cream cheese, then a generous layer of lox, then tomatoes. "Pepper?" he says. She nods enthusiastically.

When Jeff reaches for a red onion, Billy Jack calls across the cafe, "No onions!" There's a beat, and then she crumples. The fug of *No onions* hangs in the air.

Jeff puts a dill garnish on the plate of bagels and lox and brings it to Billy Jack, who has collapsed onto her journal. She scrawls, I BLEW IT.

"You and me both," he says. "I won't tell if you don't."

SOMEDAY WE'RE GONNA LAUGH ABOUT THIS, RIGHT??

Jeff sips a Bloody Mary at Sakura's Lounge. His drink is perfumed with the floral scent billowing off the fried-haired woman several bar stools away. She finishes her gimlet, then checks her makeup in a compact, reapplying coral lipstick before joining the tide of suits rushing off to work. Sakura does a slow hula. At the far end of the bar, a man strikes matches one after the other, letting them burn down to his fingertips. He twists a cocktail napkin and sets it on fire. Spidery wisps of ash dance into the air. Sakura waves her arms.

Jeff lights a Benson & Hedges Deluxe Ultra Light Menthol 100. The man at the end of the bar asks for a smoke, and Jeff says, "They're menthol."

"I like menthol," the man says. He gets up and plants himself on the stool beside Jeff, who thinks, *Cute, in a preppy sort of way.* The man's hair is brown and thick, his glasses are fashionably small wire-rims; he looks *expensive*—manicured, buffed, and bronzed—but his face is unshaven, and he has the musk of a few days without a shower. "I'm Andrew," he says. "And I'm buying you a drink."

He orders two Bloody Marys. Top-shelf. Nobody orders top-shelf at Sakura's; the vodka bottle is furred with dust. Sakura sways her hips as she pours.

"Do we know each other?" Jeff says.

Andrew says archly, "Do we?" Then he gestures to the drinks. "What, no celery?"

Sakura laughs and laughs.

Andrew pats his pockets. "Oh, terrific. I forgot my wallet."

Jeff counts out the last of his cash, thinking, *Chump, chump, chump, oui, oui, oui. I am the king of chumps.* He says, "I'm sure I know your face from somewhere."

"I'm not from around here," Andrew says. "I'm visiting a friend. You know Zanzare?"

"The designer," Jeff says, unimpressed.

"I've done walk-ons in a few movies—maybe that's where you've seen me. Did you see the remake of *Planet of the Apes?*"

"Uh, no."

Andrew says, "Maybe you know me from my modeling days.

Did you ever model? Your bones are exquisite." His knee bumps against Jeff's and stays there. "So, what do you do for money?"

"I'm a chef."

"I bet no one ever cooks for you," Andrew says. "Let's go to your place, and I'll fix you breakfast in bed."

"I don't have any food in the house."

"We'll shop."

"My place is a mess," Jeff says. This is not true. He was up till five, scouring.

Andrew hooks his finger under the cuff of Jeff's sleeve and says, "What are you scared of? Lie back and enjoy it. Surrender."

Jeff admits that he has no money, and Andrew's eyes go cold and flat. Quickly, Jeff says, "I'll get an advance from my boss. You'll wait for me?"

.   On the way to Mad Manya's, he almost trips over a dubious sidewalk sale: boomboxes, watches, jewelry, and a filthy sky-blue duffel bag. Flapping on hangers on a cyclone fence are a couple of Jeff's own shirts. And on the sidewalk is his music box. He picks it up, and the seller says, "That's five dollars."

"No, it isn't," Jeff says. "It's mine." He pulls his clothes off the cyclone fence and shoves them into his duffel bag, "Don't follow me," he says and walks away.

Jeff hears Rita in his head: *Point to yourself and say, "Temple."* He is not going back to Sakura's Lounge.

At the cafe, Billy Jack is absently sucking malted milk balls in the front window. Jeff knocks on the glass, startling Billy Jack. Malted milk balls soar and hail down around her. "Gold-berg! I got my music box!"

Jeff gets in bed with Billy Jack. He picks a malted milk ball out of the blankets and puts it in his cheek. Drew, wearing all black, calls from the counter, "Are you coming to the candle-light vigil tonight?"

Jeff says, "What candlelight vigil?"

"For Zanzare," Drew says. "He was murdered. Shot and stabbed with pruning shears, and I was just wearing a pair of Zanzare pants last night!"

Now, Jeff knows where he knows Andrew's face from. Right there in the window, the face on the wanted poster. Trembling, Jeff winds the key to his music box, and it plinks out the opening notes of "You Light Up My Life." The seagull flies in a herky-jerky figure eight. In the mirror, reflected in the pupil of his eye, is a little Jeff. And in the pupil of that little Jeff's eye, too small to see, is another Jeff, and another, and so on into infinity.

courtesy of HeeBe JeeBe photo booth, Petaluma, CA

Noria Jablonski was born in San Francisco and grew up in a commune in Petaluma, California. She received her MFA in Creative Writing from the University of Massachusetts-Amherst and her BA from the University of Northern California.

WITHDRAWAL